CHEYENNE WILLIAMS

A WESTERN

by

K. Imus

KEICO COMPANY
407 NW 132nd Street
Seattle, WA 98177

International Standard Book No. 0-9653584-2-9
Library of Congress Catalog Card # 98-94102

Imus, K., *Cheyenne Williams*

Printed in Canada

To obtain copies of *Cheyenne Williams* by K. Imus, contact your local bookstore, library, or write to the Keico Company. Other books by K. Imus, *Zero Smith* (ISBN 0-96535840-2) and *Galway* (ISBN 0-9653584-1-0) are also available.

Cover design by Andre' Potgieter
Photo of K. Imus by Rene Salmon

Published
by

KEICO COMPANY
407 NW 132nd Street
Seattle, WA 98177
Fax: 206-361-6249
E-mail: keithimus@aol.com

DEDICATION

To a woman

from

ANYWHERE

Books by K. Imus

ZERO SMITH
ISBN 0-9653584-0-2
$6.95

GALWAY
ISBN 0-9653584-1-0
$8.95

CHEYENNE WILLIAMS
ISBN 0-9653584-2-9
$6.95

Copies of K. Imus' books can be ordered from bookstores or directly from Keico Company,
407 NW 132nd Street, Seattle, WA 98177
Fax: 206-361-6249
E-mail: keithimus@aol.com

CHEYENNE WILLIAMS

A Western

"Guns frequently misfire,
but knives never do.
They are always as accurate
as your skill."

Advice to Cheyenne
from his Grandfather
1846

"LEARN TO LISTEN TO THE CROW"

K. Imus

1960

BOOK ONE

THE PRODIGY

CHAPTER ONE

Cheyenne Williams was a plainsman. He was also a selfish man. He was all man in the physical sense, being taller and stronger than most men are. Williams was a rascal with a sense of humor, which frequently got him into trouble. One of the troubles was that women wanted him, and quite frequently, so did their husbands, but for different reasons, of course, and occasionally so did the law.

Cheyenne Williams liked being wanted by women but took a dim view of husbands in general and the law in particular. Occasionally, he was wanted by both at the same time. This made him uncomfortable. He looked with a jaundiced eye on any one attempting to thwart his selfish pursuits where women were concerned. If the lady was willing, that was all that mattered.

Williams never really cared much for most men. He thought the West had far too many men, anyway. He was not sympathetic toward much of anything that men wanted.

With the slightest provocation, Cheyenne pounded on them viciously and often.

When he did, he was not a nice man. He nearly always broke something: noses, fingers, arms, ribs, and occasionally heads.

Williams was a mixed blood of an unusual combination. He was Indian, black, white and Hawaiian. It was difficult to tell just what his ancestry was and he had learned early in life, if he chose, to verbally persuade any race that he was one of them. In New Orleans he could and did pass for a quadroon, which in fact he nearly was. He even learned some of the speech patterns.

In the Alamo country, most folks would assume that he was part, if not all, Mexican. In the Kansas territory, most white folks assumed he was mostly white with perhaps some Indian blood and as for the Indians, they assumed that he was at least a half-breed, which he nearly was. He was also very smart and had a flair for picking up languages. He spoke several Indian dialects and was good at sign language. His Spanish was just fair but his English was that of a reasonably well-educated man.

His academic education was the result of a few years in a mission school during his youth and an exposure to a lot of books, plus the tireless and nearly Herculean tutoring efforts of a gorgeous, young English teacher named Miss Moresby. The lass diligently pressed her insatiable charms and many varied skills upon the handsome young Adonis. To his credit, young Williams never tired of these endless tutoring sessions, and in spite of many interruptions away from the printed word, he learned a rather high level of English grammar and vocabulary.

He read Johnson and Coleridge, Kiam and Keats, Emerson, Thoreau and Moresby. He read a lot of Moresby, from most every angle. When he learned to pun, he often referred to her as his "open book of epic proportions." She certainly had epic proportions. Her body was spectacular. So was her insatiable interest and appetite. She might have single handedly exhausted Caesar's legions.

Among his other readings was a book called "The Western Savage," written by an idiot. The author's narrow Calvinist view saw the Indian as "Satan's Pawn" because the Indian was enjoying life in this world instead of preparing for the next one. The heathen savages danced, fornicated, and celebrated life, and every one knows just how evil that sort of thing can be.

Williams had spent most of his adult life trying to get it right and then this Calvinist came along and tried to rain on his parade.

Williams was right, the guy was an idiot, so like any sensible reader, he threw the book away. He was also right in assuming the author had never seen an Indian; it was true. The man had not.

Cheyenne Williams was born handsome and he became even better looking as he matured. The color of his eyes was an unusual mixture. They were light-gray and yellow-amber colored, which were very wolf-like. His skin was caramel colored, rather like coffee with lots of cream. He had thick, long, black, wavy hair that was usually tied with red wool ribbon, made by some far off southwest tribe. His bright smile showed perfect white teeth set in a strong square jaw. In addition Cheyenne Williams had a muscular, sinewy body, very heavy in the shoulders, yet lean everywhere else, and he had big hands and feet. He also had an unusually deep resonant voice and he laughed easily. Women considered Cheyenne Williams extraordinarily handsome and marvelously endowed, which was a very dangerous combination. Cheyenne being a lusty sort of man, spent a good deal of his time thinking about women. He considered them often. A quick glance at a woman and he pretty well knew what she would look like in the buff. Williams was a man who loved women, but he was partial to what the world called the "Rubenesque" type. His word for the same type was "ripe." He was a man who needed women so he worked diligently in that endeavor. Women were the "icing on his cake of life."

We have all heard of the child's evening prayer that starts out, "Now I lay me, etc." Williams's only prayer was a derivative of that and it was adaptable to any time of day. It said simply, "I hope I get laid."

Sometimes there was this awkwardness. The woman was willing but she was also married. With husbands wearing guns, their wives were often a dangerous prospect. It made for a dicey condition because Cheyenne Williams was also dangerous. Occasionally, to the regret of some of these husbands, he was lethal.

Cheyenne Williams had a quick temper, incredible skill with his many weapons, including several knives, a Colt .44 replaced just this week by the new Remington .44 top strap cartridge model pistol. (His main reason for going to St. Louis.)

Williams would be formidable with his new weapons and his lightning draw because he was an excellent shot.

Quite naturally he solved these difficult

problems with a mixture of cold ferocity, amazing speed, animal viciousness, and always with the utmost dispatch. He didn't care for loose ends. He frequently said, "Loose ends can come back to try and kill you."

Cheyenne Williams loved women. He had the unique ability to always be in love with the girl he was with at the time. At first, they were Indian women because he grew up in a Cheyenne village. Later, he was captured by the U.S. Cavalry and sent to a Mission school. At the age of fourteen, he learned about white women, much to his joy. When he escaped back to his own people at age fifteen, he found he wanted more of both worlds; the white man's world and the Indian's world as well, and he began to drift back and forth until he learned to be comfortable in both camps.

Because he lived life on the wild side, it was often very advantageous to slide in or out of the Indian or the white world, depending on whose laws he'd broken. It also depended on who and how many were chasing him.

He discovered early on that women were pretty much the same except some were hornier than others. They dressed differently, not just from men, but differently from each other.

White women wore all kinds of under garments while Indian women wore very little, if anything, under the garment that one saw. Williams preferred the Indian way of dress.

He was in trouble again and it happened this way. This week's trouble was killing trouble and for the usual reasons. He'd shot up the town's favorite son and the law was intending to come down on him "with all fours," when we find out who the perpetrators of these vile misdeeds is-are-were, as they put it, and if they could catch him-them, which wasn't likely. The prudent move for Cheyenne was to hightail it to the "high lonesome." So he did that.

The entire affair was really just that, an affair. The town's favorite son was a young political type.

"A real comer," they said.

"He might even become President someday."

Well, it seems this political type paid a whole lot of attention to the public welfare but neglected the private welfare of his very fancy lady, who's name was Maribelle McFadden.

One evening, this high spirited lass was very disenchanted with local politics and was feeling sorry for herself, when she noticed a very handsome man staring at her.

Usually Cheyenne Williams had the look of a plainsman but not today. Williams was all cleaned up for a change. He'd had a bath, was wearing new store-bought clothes and was carrying only one concealed knife instead of the usual three. He was wearing a six gun as were a few other men, when he walked into the hotel dining room and noticed this beauty, seated there.

They looked intently at each other and both looked as if they were a huge cat looking at a small tethered mouse. Cheyenne bought dinner for the lady and afterward, quite naturally, he wouldn't think of allowing her to return to her room unescorted in this savage land.

He explained, "While most folks were decent enough, this was after all, still the frontier and anything could happen." And of course it did, much to their mutual delight.

It was the farthest west the lady had ever been and the farthest east he cared to go. He didn't much like her world but he didn't tell her that. He was here to buy three new Remington pistols, which he did.

He was even further east than was prudent to go because of the prevalence of the law and the fact that he'd learned his rowdy behavior was frowned on in most of the "settlements," Cheyenne's word for cities and towns.

Breaking heads, cutting up the citizens and a shooting now and then, tasks at which Cheyenne Williams had acquired considerable skill, were viewed with a jaundiced eye in the "settlements."

This "settlement" was actually Saint Louis, Missouri. The place was so tame, Cheyenne figured that one concealed knife and a six- gun would be enough armament for this burg and he was right. He also figured it would be no time at all before they put in gas street lamps, even to the out-skirts of town. This later proved to be true.

The spirited Maribelle loved what she called the animal quality of Cheyenne, yet it was she who left scratches on his back and a bite bruise here and there. She also called him her "Knight Errant." Who was he to argue at such a critical time?

Maribelle McFadden was an exceedingly fair damsel and she was very definitely in great distress, or was, until she met Cheyenne Williams.

"You did come to my rescue, you know. I was so bored."

Cheyenne thought to himself, the word "bored" was her euphemism for horny. She was certainly "bored" all right, in many ways.

It seemed to him that he was the one in distress. His body was covered with lusty, though superficial wounds, administered to him by the fair damsel, Maribelle, as he rescued her over and over again.

Maribelle had performed in a style of which any classy whorehouse madam would have been more than proud. He had mostly hung on as they went on their mercurial rides. It was better than great. One might say it was even "Homeric."

When it was over they were each wearing a big dumb grin. She was all perky, bright eyed and bushy-tailed and he was thoroughly wrung out. She was raring to go and he could hardly move. The big grins were the kind that you get in only one way and still showed when "Mister Political" returned from making speeches two days later.

The situation was slightly awkward, even though fortunately for them, they were in the dining room of the hotel when the man arrived.

Maribelle introduced Cheyenne to the "Political" and when she turned to introduce the "Political" to Cheyenne she could not for the life of her, remember her fiancé's name.

At that moment nobody cared except the "Political." He had a vague idea that he had been insulted and he couldn't hit a lady, so he swung at Cheyenne, which was the worst mistake the man ever made. Cheyenne decked him instantly which was followed by a "little over-reaction." Cheyenne kicked him very hard in the groin, and the Political responded immediately by vomiting his innards and two of his front teeth all over himself. Next Cheyenne put his knee in the man's chest so hard he cracked two ribs away from the man's sternum. Then he held the biggest knife the "Political" had ever seen, to the man's throat. The man's lightning, macho response was to go immediately into shock. A good thing he did, or Cheyenne might have killed him. As it was, the fool Political aspirant had more than a slight skin cut across his throat where the razor sharp knife touched him and he had blood and vomit in his hair, on his shirt, his suit and the hotel dinning room carpet.

Maribelle had mixed emotions. She wasn't quite sure whom to root for, her meal ticket, or the best lover she had ever known. She was smart enough to know that her Political type was a pompous ass on occasion, and probably deserved some of the treatment he got, but he would still be here long after Cheyenne Williams was gone.

Cheyenne saw her to her room and then he spent the night in the park—a good thing because the Political hired thugs to bomb his room.

The explosion was so powerful, it even blew out a wall. A married guy next door was there for a quickie with his secretary. The timing was perfect and when the wall harmlessly burst in on them, she was wide-eyed, mute, and grinning from ear to ear, and all the married guy could say was, "Jesus Christ."

As usual, the police made it awkward with questions no one wanted to answer.

The next day Cheyenne went to Maribelle's room to say good-bye to Maribelle and instead was met by the Political and a tin horn gunman. Both men drew guns on Cheyenne. Big mistake! Cheyenne threw two of his knives at the same time and quietly put their lights out.

Cheyenne went to the livery stable where he changed his clothes from businessman to a buckskin clad plainsman. He divided his hair into two long clumps and wrapped each clump with red ribbon, placed an eagle feather on his flat crowned leather hat and quietly rode out of town in broad daylight.

Wearing his smoke stained old buckskins, he reasoned correctly that no one would look for him in that outfit. He was also wearing Apache moccasins with a throwing knife in each one, and two .44 caliber six guns belted around his waist. In addition, he carried a big knife that he had out of sight at the moment. Cheyenne Williams was riding a big, mean Appaloosa stallion and he very much looked like a plainsman who had just come to town. He was as inconspicuous as a lamb in a wolf pack, but he looked nothing like the gentleman that had checked into the fancy hotel.

Cheyenne slowly walked his horse to the edge of town and once there, rode like hell for the open country. No one would be looking for a plainsman. And they didn't.

Days later, upon discovery of the bodies, the hotel people called the law.

Cheyenne had gone to St. Louis to have a look around and stay in one of those fancy hotels. Now here he was headed west again, heading out for his kind of country. It hadn't been a bad five days. He was looking forward to the open country; he needed a rest to get his strength back.

He was also looking back in his mind at the lusty damsel, Maribelle McFadden. He was smiling to himself and vowed to see her again if possible. He might even consider sending for her. It seemed a good idea at the time.

Cheyenne

CHAPTER TWO

Occasionally, Williams did the chameleon role. He changed his "spots" to suit his purpose. He was never the polished sophisticate, but he did the business man role well enough, and he could fall into the western rancher role very easily. He also fell into the feathered Cheyenne warrior role, or frontier plainsman role, in the blink of an eye, as in this case.

He usually dressed as a plainsman even when he did cowhand work, which meant he wore a buckskin outfit, top to bottom. He wore a wide brimmed, flat crowned, black hat low over the eyes, which often gave him a rather sinister look. He was taller than most men are and the hat made him seem even taller.

This day Cheyenne was armed to the teeth. He wore Apache legging moccasins, with a throwing knife sewn in each one with the tip of the blades showing on the outside. He had a huge knife on his belt and a six gun in a lightweight, elk hide holster, tied low to his right leg as usual, but today there was more. Behind his big elk horn buckle was a double-barreled .44 Derringer. In addition to all of this hardware he was also carrying a flat eleven-inch throwing knife, worn in a flat sheath that hung down his back, under his shirt. The man bristled with armament. He called it "being prepared." The main reason for all the armament was that he was riding west and alone through an unkind world.

Like most Indians, he wore a medicine bag. It hung high on his chest on a light thong around his neck. The medicine bags were usually filled with assorted goodies such as bones, feathers, a piece of fur or hair, maybe even a pebble, to protect the Indians from evil spirits. However, unlike his Indian blood brothers, Cheyenne's medicine bag was filled with nuggets, gold ones, to protect him from poverty and so he could buy spirits.

He owned an angry horse and a worn saddle. The saddle carried two saddle guns and a rifle. The saddle guns were like the new handgun on his leg, a Remington top strap with revolving cylinders that took the new .44 cartridges. He'd bought the new guns in St. Louis.

Williams was a calm and smiling man

but he did have a short fuse if angered. If he wasn't smiling, his eyes frequently had a sinister look under normal conditions. When angered, he looked positively crazed.

He could conjure up a look so evil and mean, that one fellow commented, "When Cheyenne looks like that, even a grizzly bear would get up and give Cheyenne his chair."

In a fight he was something to behold. No one that was an eyewitness to one of his fights ever challenged Cheyenne Williams, no matter what the circumstance.

Once he was attacked by a band of Blackfeet warriors who were painted for war. He killed all thirteen of them and received only a slight scratch himself. He shot eight, threw knives at four and broke the neck of the last one. He left his mark which was a "W" carved on the chest of several of the dead warriors, but he didn't take any scalps.

"Wims"—that's what the Indians called him—was much respected and even admired for this, even by his enemies, because leaving them their scalps allowed the dead to cross over to the spirit world and join the Star People. It also sent a message to his enemies that he had such strong medicine he didn't need the medicine in the scalps of the dead warriors to give him strength. "Wims" was greatly admired as a warrior.

Cheyenne

His reputation preceded him in both the red and white world and grew with each new exploit. The Indians told stories of "Wims," the great warrior of the Cheyenne, who could sometimes live among the whites, their enemy, because his medicine was so strong. In the white man's world he had even stronger medicine. He had gold. With it came respect, but too often, also came someone, attempting to steal it from him. So far, it had always resulted in the deaths of the thieves.

Most people didn't recognize Cheyenne Williams as a gunfighter because he looked more like a mountain man than a gunfighter. Also, he spent much of his life out in the open country where there weren't many people. The whites taught him to read so when he went to the "settlements," as he called them, for supplies, he bought books along with the usual stuff. He went to the settlements for another reason as well, for women, which he also called "supplies."

The average time of abstinence of the western man did not appeal to this lusty plainsman. Cheyenne Williams had a high interest in the frequency of "supplies."

CHAPTER THREE

Williams had traveled well into the vast, rolling grasslands of the western Kansas territory where he came across a cattle drive. It was a Texas trail outfit that needed help with its herd of about three thousand head. Cheyenne signed on. They were headed for Abilene.

Things went along fine for a few days until a testy top hand didn't like the way Williams was bringing along the remuda. The horses were sweated up some because Cheyenne had hurried them along after he'd stopped to climb aboard a bronc. The horse was giving one of the younger cowboys a bad time whenever the lad tried to saddle up.

Cheyenne roped the bronc tight to a big rock and saddled and unsaddled and then saddled him again. Each time he saddled he climbed aboard and talked to the horse to calm the critter. Within a few minutes the horse was getting the message. The other wrangler thought it was a neat piece of work.

When the lesson was over, Cheyenne and the wrangler brought along the remuda to catch up with the herd. True enough they were lathered a little, but now there was a safer horse in the bunch and the kid could probably saddle up in the morning without risking life and limb. When the top hand got mouthy with Cheyenne, Cheyenne simply rode away, or started to. The next thing he felt was a whip across his back. Some of the drovers had whips with them to push the herds. It was a mistake because Cheyenne turned, grabbed the end of the whip and jerked Mr. "top-hand" right out of the saddle. The man landed hard on the ground on his back and Cheyenne landed on the man with both feet, cracking his ribs and rearranging his insides. Cheyenne hit the man in the mouth just before the man vomited. There were teeth and assorted horribles all over the ground. Cheyenne was strangling the top hand with his own whip when two cowboys put lariats around him and pulled him off. The men were all set to drag Cheyenne off into the sunset. After all, no breed could do that to one of their Texas buddies and live to tell about it.

A second later both men had their hands in the air because Cheyenne had cut away the ropes and had a gun on the men so fast they just couldn't believe it.

"That's enough, man," shouted one of the ropers.

"We give up."

"Throw your guns over here, climb down, and take your boots off."

When the men were disarmed Cheyenne picked up their guns and put them in his saddlebag. One of the cowhands carried a nine-inch knife, which Cheyenne took. He tied their boots to his saddle. Taking their horses, he climbed aboard the big stallion and pushed the remuda with him. When he arrived back at the chuck wagon where the "big auger," boss man was, he asked for his time and left the outfit.

As he was riding out he dropped off two pair of boots near the chuck wagon. The cowhands standing around just stared at the boots, stupefied.

Cheyenne Williams was smiling as he rode away, thinking of those boys walking all the way back to the night camp in their stocking feet. It was about four miles, through rock, thorns, scrub brush and even some small ground cactus. He really didn't care if the third man made it back or not. He had the fellows whip and was quite pleased with himself.

Cheyenne

CHAPTER FOUR

Williams figured he'd been on the trail long enough. It was actually a little under three weeks since his time with Maribelle and he figured he was over due for "supplies." Three weeks in the West was not a long time for cowhands to go without a woman. Some trail drives were four to six months long with no towns in between. Cheyenne Williams was not willing to speak for other men, but he was of the opinion celibacy was for priests. To Cheyenne's way of thinking, to be without a woman for three weeks was two and a half weeks too long. The longer he was away from women, the nastier his disposition. Abstinence made him downright dangerous. For this reason, he tended to look for work, for short periods of time, where there were women, and lots of them. That meant towns. He was a fair gambler, and that meant the bigger towns of the West.

He usually kept moving, because he was in one scrape after another. He called it "keeping sharp."

The disadvantage of this life style was that his reputation as a lover, scoundrel and gunman, in the reverse order, preceded him.

The very thought of "rescuing" another fair damsel in the next settlement lent a certain excitement to his daily life. Because he had the unusual gift of always being thoroughly in love with the woman with whom he was playing, they seemed to like the idea and it gave Cheyenne Williams, for brief periods at least, a certain peace of mind, unless the women were married. Then, of course, these affairs occasionally became awkward.

Williams, who really didn't care for this sort of thing, figured it was a lot like picking up the check. It was just part of the game. One had to pay dues sometimes.

Cheyenne rode across a high bluff just at sunset. He climbed down to rest his horse and watch the sun go down. There were huge clouds that were turning all shades of color, such as pink, coral, lavender, and red-orange. There was gold at the edges of the clouds high up and a cream color on those clouds that were way off to the southwest. A large area of light blue sky edged the clouds. As the sun lowered to the horizon, the sky turned red-orange and scarlet with many purple hues. The colors continued to darken as he rode toward town.

Cheyenne Williams wondered if any one in Turkey Flats was watching this magnificent sunset at the same time that he was. Down there they wouldn't see the sun itself, this late in the day, but they could certainly still see the sky.

The big deep blue dome of the sky was turning dark behind him as he rode down off the bluff expecting to find the town of Turkey Flats. He hoped the town would be better than the name implied as he looked at the battered, shot-up sign, which was hanging precariously by one end on a slanting old post. The few lights he saw didn't lend much encouragement.

He rode down the main drag and in twilight the town looked tired. He tilted his head to read a cock-eyed dirty sign hanging by only one nail that said, "Hosses for rent and sale." It occurred to Williams that this town certainly needed a sign painter.

He rode the big Appaloosa stud right into an empty stall, unsaddled, and was rubbing him down when a dried up ancient, with a face wrinkled like a walnut, said in a crackling voice, "Hey, you can't."

Cheyenne put his big paw around the ancient's scrawny neck and lifted the man right up off the ground with one hand. He carried the little man, hands and feet dangling, over under the light in this manner and held him there. Evil eye ball, to eye ball, "You were saying."

"Any stall you like," squeaked the man.

"Stay away from that horse. He'll kill you. I'll attend to him, myself. Make a sign so others keep away."

Carrying his saddlebags and his rifle, Cheyenne walked to what in this town, passed for a hotel. The only noise in town was from the bar across the street.

The hotel clerk turned the register around so Cheyenne could sign it. Cheyenne looked him in the eye and said, "Just give me the key, send up a bath and a bottle of your best whiskey."

The nice man had big, round, frightened eyes by this time and he gave Cheyenne his key with a trembling hand. He was quite sure that this was the most terrifying human being he had ever seen in his life. The little clerk was more right than he suspected.

Cheyenne Williams went to his room.

CHAPTER FIVE

The room, like the tired town and the even more tired hotel, was certainly a come-down compared to the fancy hotel in St. Louis. He had spent a good part of his adult life living in hotels in the west similar to this one, but this place was drearier than anything he'd seen before. He was sure that it crawled. It had a worn lock on a flimsy door that could be opened with a penknife or a slight kick and a stained and cracked mirror above the dresser. The room was papered with grubby, aged, striped wallpaper that made the tall ceiling seem even higher than it was. The bed, like those in cheap hotels everywhere, sagged in the middle. The sheets, if they could be called that, looked as though they had been used many times without being washed.

His room was a dump. Williams glanced around the room and went back downstairs, grabbed the nervous little clerk by his stained suit front and half lifted him over the counter.

He said, "This hell hole is a fire trap. Clean it up or I'll come back and burn it to the ground."

Cheyenne left carrying his gear as he crossed to the saloon.

He walked out, preferring the prairie if necessary, to the wretched hotel. It seemed prudent to try to spend the night in nicer surroundings and, to Cheyenne Williams, that meant he should try and find some feminine companionship. There was probably a local bawdyhouse, or as a last resort, even the prairie.

The hotel had only the one name, "Hotel," and the saloon name was equally succinct. It was labeled "Saloon," which implied it was the only one in town. Well, one ought to be enough, he thought.

The weather had turned bad just as Cheyenne rode in. By now there was a cold wind pushing a hard, steady rain.

Williams plowed his way through the mud and manure toward the saloon, putting him in an even nastier mood than the one he was in already from dealing with the sleazy clerk, in that crummy pest-hole, hotel.

Cheyenne barged up to the bar.

"Whiskey in a bottle."

When it was placed on the bar, Cheyenne put his big hand around it. Pulling the cork with his teeth, he walked over to the main source of heat, a pot bellied stove that was surrounded by a few of the locals. There were men playing poker at one of the tables nearby.

The place smelled like all saloons: stale cigar smoke, yesterdays' booze and unwashed men. As if that were not enough, tonight the saloon had the added smell of rank, wet wool clothes.

On this foul night, it seemed a cozy haven against the rain and the oncoming storm. Williams drank from the bottle and felt the burn all the way down. Two more belts and he felt better.

There was the smell of food coming from the next room. After a while he wandered in and ordered dinner from a slovenly Indian waitress. Her dress was stain covered and her hair was a wild tangle. She looked to be without hope and apparently was. Cheyenne looked closer when she brought his coffee. He thought to himself that she might look all right if someone cleaned her up. The meal was barely edible, but the coffee was good.

When dinner was over, the girl cleared the table and in the process dropped a dish. A man came charging out from the kitchen yelling and slapped the girl two times before Cheyenne caught the man's hand in midstrike. Cheyenne forced the man to the floor as he crushed his hand. Cheyenne slowly squeezed the hand until the bones collapsed. The man screamed and fainted.

"Girl, what is he to you?"

"He's my father's brother and he hates me because I'm part Indian."

"Then he probably hates me because I'm also part Indian."

The girl continued, "Unlike him, my father was a wonderful man. We lived wild and free, trapping. Then the Blackfeet killed my parents about four months ago, and the U.S. Army brought me here to be a work slave for that horrible man. I am half Crow but I have no people now. I belong to no Indian village and with the whites, I am an outcast. I stay dirty and uncombed so the young men will leave me alone. Thank you for helping me. Sometimes he keeps hitting me until I am unconscious."

The man on the floor was coming around. He had difficulty getting up from the floor. Still getting up, when he was bent over, Cheyenne kicked his backside and launched him out the door. Struggling to keep his balance, he was last seen running down the street. It wasn't difficult to tell where he was going.

"Get your things. You are coming with

me."

"I have nothing."

"You will have. I guarantee it."

"Do you have any wages coming?"

"I don't know. He never paid me any thing. I get left over food from the plates of the customers and I sleep on the floor in a closet in the back."

"Where is the cash?"

The girl showed him. Cheyenne took what he thought was about three months' wages and a fat bonus for the girl. Then he promised to get her a bath and some clothes.

Before they could leave, they were both stopped by the Sheriff and a couple of the locals. Coming in the door was good old uncle "what's his name."

"Now hold on, Sheriff, we don't want any trouble. This girl is my sister and I'm taking her out of here. The fool that runs this dump," nodding toward the uncle, "was beating on her when I stopped him."

Cheyenne added, "She has worked here three months and without any wages, and the only food she has been eating is table scraps. Her boss ought to be horse whipped. How could you allow a thing like this to happen in your town?"

The Sheriff scowled at the uncle and said, "Is this true, Ed?"

"Would you take the word of a couple of redskins before you'd take mine?"

"Ed, you've been on the sorry side for a long time. You know this isn't the first complaint I've had about the way you treat your help. When those cowhands molested the girl you did nothing to stop it."

"Sheriff, if she leaves, I got nobody to help me and I can't cook with a busted hand," he whined.

"You two walk with me over to my office."

"Sheriff, is there a decent place for the girl to get cleaned up?"

"Ma Sullivan's rooming house isn't too bad and she'll take Indians if you can pay. Just down the street on the left. Food's good, too."

"Thanks, Sheriff."

CHAPTER SIX

Ma Sullivan was round and jolly. She looked like she might double for Mrs. Claus during the holidays.

"We want two rooms for a day or two."

"Only got one left, take it or leave it."

"You got a bath tub, some soap, some towels and a comb?"

"Yes, it's extra, but I'll throw in some cold chicken."

Cheyenne nodded.

"That'll be a dollar and a half in advance. The water will be ready in about twenty minutes," she said, giving them the key and pointing out the room and the tub out back.

Cheyenne and the girl settled into the room. He had whiskey and she went out to have a bath. He was thinking, what have I got myself into, adopting a squaw who has no folks. Why, she doesn't even have any trade goods, he thought humorously. And more seriously, it occurred to him that she didn't have a horse or an anything.

After more whiskey, he went out to the bathhouse to have a look at the girl. To his surprise he discovered that she was no longer a girl but rather a very attractive young girl-woman. On second thought, he conceded she did have some things.

She had a slim, rib showing body with ripe looking, pretty high breasts and long, strong legs. All of this, and yet a kind of child's innocence. She was perplexing; not the sort of earthy animal that Cheyenne preferred.

Well, there goes the evening, he thought, but I might as well bathe as long as I'm here. He undressed. Instead of the girl getting out, she moved over to make room for her new protector. To Cheyenne, she seemed altogether too obedient. As she finished washing her hair, Cheyenne said, "Out you go, lass. It's my turn to scrub down."

She got out of the tub and dried herself while he watched, and then she said, "I don't have any clothes to wear."

"I've brought you one of my shirts to wear until tomorrow when the stores are open. It's the best I can do for now."

When the girl put the shirt on she didn't have any hands. The sleeves flapped loosely beyond her fingertips. It would have been comical if she wasn't so beautiful. The shoulder seam of the shirt came to her elbows and the shirttail came almost to her mid thigh. The girl smiled and said, "I bet I look funny."

Cheyenne doubted she had any idea that she was such a gorgeous eyeful, but he said, "Not quite."

The girl dried her hair as they talked.

Williams was in the tub drinking whiskey. They both acted as though they did this every Saturday night. He was used to having things his way and she was a stoic and seemed to endure without question. Cheyenne made a mental note to consider the fact that a little change in both of them might make them into better people.

"What do you intend to do with me, Mr. Williams?"

"You got it wrong girl. From now on you are your own boss and don't let anyone push you around ever again. I'll help you get situated somewhere and then I'll be on my way cause I have a lot of things to do. We'll find you a decent job somewhere and a clean place to live, and you'll be off and running before you know it."

Thinking to himself, what did he have to do that was so important? Come to think of it, nothing he had ever done was important, except perhaps the time when he helped Zero Smith during the Pinedale War.

Instead of feeling saddled with the girl,

he might think of this as a chance to help her, to do something for someone else for a change. Until now, he hadn't even asked her name. He'd been calling her girl as though she were an object. Well, he could fix that.

Cheyenne was taking a new look at himself. Compassion was not high on the list of Cheyenne Williams' emotions. He was a survivor, which meant selfish. He cared about his own creature comforts and, of course, the ladies. He was more than a little crazed when some clown attempted to interfere with his pursuit of those comforts. Otherwise, he was mostly honest and minded his own business.

Maybe it was because this little girl was a "breed," like him, and seemed so helpless, that he was assuming the roll of protector. She hadn't even asked for his help. Life would be hard for her here in the white man's world, just as it had been for him at first.

/////////////

Looking back, Cheyenne was grateful to his grandfather for insisting that he learn about knife throwing. He had hunted with knives. He could hit a sparrow at thirty feet. He recalled his Grandfather saying, "Guns misfire but knives never do; they are as reliable as your skill."

Coming out of his reverie he thought perhaps he should teach her the knife.

"What's your name, Miss?"

"I wondered if you would ever ask me?"

"I have two names, actually. My father called me "Little Kitten" and my name with my mother's people is "Morning Flower."

"You aren't so little any more. I'll call you "Kitten."

"We'll feed you tomorrow along with getting you new clothes, but for now, have some of this chicken and a drink if you care to.

She tried some of each. It was her first drink. She couldn't believe how awful it was.

"It's an acquired taste," he said, smiling his bright smile and taking another big jolt.

She thought him beautiful.

Williams was still in the tub and the girl was fluffing her long black hair as she dried it.

"Kitten, you sure are nice to look at when you are all cleaned up."

She beamed all over. It was the first nice thing anyone had said to her since before her parents were killed.

"I didn't think I would ever be clean again. It feels wonderful. I used to roll in the dirt and put dirt in my hair so men would leave me alone. You'd be surprised what a barrier dirt can be."

"You need more protection than dirt. How would you like to learn the knife? I can teach you to throw and to fight in close. I could teach you the six gun, but they are damn heavy and it's not exactly lady like to wear a gun."

"Is it lady like to carry a knife?"

"Not just one knife, Kitten, two or three. One sheathed down your back, one strapped to the inside of your leg and one up your sleeve. With all of that you could hold off an army."

"Why can't I learn both knives and guns? There were times when I have wished that I could shoot."

"Oh, when was that?"

"When those two cowboys molested me."

"What do you mean by molested?"

"I was raped. It was after that, that I decided to roll in the dirt."

The look on Cheyenne's face changed dramatically.

"Did you tell you uncle."

"He just smirked."

"Are those boys still around?"

"Yes, they are brothers and their Pa is one of the biggest ranchers around here, so they do pretty much as they please."

"How often do they come to town?"

"Two or three times a week and always

on Saturday."

"I'd like to meet those two."

"If you stick around this town you will, cause they don't like breeds and they are always looking for trouble. Oh, you will meet them, all right."

Cheyenne got out of the bath. The girl watched with some interest.

"You have scars," she said.

As he turned she noticed the whipping scars on his back and a long knife scar over most of his left ribs.

Cheyenne didn't say anything, but he did think to himself that the people who did this to him were all dead, and he smiled an enigmatic smile that she couldn't read.

As he dressed, he wondered if this hick town had the kind of knives the girl would need. If not, she could use one of his. He also thought now that she should learn guns. He always had extra guns and ammo.

"Kitten, your training starts tomorrow. It will be tough at first but just remember why you are learning these skills, so you can be your own boss, so no one can push you around ever again. You keep remembering that and you'll learn fast. You are going to have very sore hands, but it will be worth it. A month from now you will be a different person."

"By the way, Kitten, how old are you?"
"Sixteen."

CHAPTER SEVEN

When they got to the room Cheyenne said, "You take the bed and I'll sleep on the floor."

She replied, "I won't bite you. You can sleep on the bed."

"It's too soft for me, I sleep better on the ground, or in this case, the floor."

Within ten minutes, the girl was sound asleep and Cheyenne moved from there like a shadow. He went back to that sleazy restaurant that was owned by the girl's uncle, broke in and, just as he figured, the tightwad was too cheap to live anywhere else. He found him snoring in the back in a dingy room.

Cheyenne hauled him out of bed and slapped him around in the dark until his hands ached, and then he slapped him some more. The man collapsed on the floor and Cheyenne left like a shadow.

He went to the saloon, had two drinks and a lady.

Later, she asked, "Why are you hands so swollen?"

"Bee stings."

When he left, he was smiling.

Walking back, he thought of that miserable wretch and didn't really care if he died. He'd slapped him to keep from killing the son-of-a-bitch. He didn't want the Sheriff to get his nose out of joint if he was going to hang around town for a while.

He was back at Ma Sullivan's in an hour and a half with some of his anger dissipated. He slept on the floor and he slept well.

CHAPTER EIGHT

Very early the next morning, Cheyenne and the girl saddled the big Appy stud and rode double about two miles out from town. They found a place off the road with good grass for the stallion.

Cheyenne peeled the leather, and walked another quarter mile out and started gun practice. At first, he started her with an empty gun. The girl was so slim that his holster wouldn't fit her, so he punched another hole in the leather just for her.

"It's so heavy."

"That's a Remington top strap .44 caliber revolver," he said. "After a while it will seem light to you. That gun is actually lighter than most because I've had the barrel shortened about a half inch and the front sight removed. Now strap it on low."

She looked at him, and he said, "Lower. That's better."

"Now slowly draw. Again. "Now do it a hundred times. Keep careful track. Stand with your back to the sun whenever possible and try to increase you speed after the first fifty times."

He went over and sat down against a tree trunk. She had his holster, but not his favorite gun. It was tucked in his belt. He believed in being prepared. Too many pilgrims were "under" because of this harsh land.

There wasn't any law between towns and half of the towns didn't have a sheriff. They either couldn't afford it or they couldn't keep one alive long enough to clean up the place. Miles City, Dodge, Abilene and Tombstone all had that problem, along with many other towns.

She came to him and he could see the sweat on her brow and the moisture on her upper lip.

"I'm finished. My arm feels like it will fall off."

"OK, now do it again."

When she had done that, he said, "Most men have not drawn a gun more than a hundred times in their whole lives. Only the shootists have, and you are going to be one of them. That's so you can be comfortable wherever you go."

"Is your right arm tired?"

"Very."

Cheyenne had two sizable rocks that he suddenly tossed to the girl. She caught one in each hand. If she had missed they would have hurt. From this he inferred that she was at least partly ambidextrous. It was a point in her favor.

"You will learn to throw the knife with your left hand at first. Now watch me. Picking the biggest cottonwood tree he could find, his knife appeared from nowhere and stuck in the tree twenty feet away.

"You can learn to throw a knife, blade first or handle first, but once you start you can't easily change back to the other way. I suggest you learn by throwing the blade first, because the blades are very similar in the way they feel, but many handles are clumsy or poorly designed for throwing. If you move up to a bigger knife the blade will still feel the same as the small knife and it will throw almost the same.

"Now you try it. You have to count the number of turns in your mind the knife makes in a given distance. But for now, just try to hit the tree with either end and remember the blade always slides out of your hand the same way every time. It's sharp, so be a little careful. Tomorrow I'll have one filed dull so you won't cut yourself."

She practiced until she could hit the tree

almost every time. She hit the tree with the handle, with the side of the knife and occasionally with the point, but never straight on so it would stick. Cheyenne rolled his eyes upward, cringed, and looked the other way.

Then she backed up a little farther to about fifteen feet and she began to stick it sometimes. When she did she beamed. As the distance increased she found that she could see the turn of the knife in her mind more clearly. She could, of course, see some of the spin if she threw it slowly, but to be an effective weapon the knife must be thrown with force and speed. She practiced while Cheyenne brought the horse close to act as a watchdog while he had a nap. The horse always nickered if there was anything near that wasn't part of the natural scene.

In the past that had included, on separate occasions, a nasty bull, a grizzly bear, and some assorted bad guys. Cheyenne had complete faith in the horse and justifiably so. The animal had saved his bacon several times.

When Cheyenne awoke the girl was still throwing the knife and her hand was bleeding. He threw the same two rocks and she caught them the same way, one in each hand. He thought she has very quick reflexes and very quick hands. He was pleased and he told her so. She beamed.

"That's enough for today. Let me see your hands," he said, eyeing his own hands. The swelling was almost gone and by tomorrow he could shake hands with the sheriff if he had to. His hands were the reason they left town so early without all of the knives they would need. He wanted them back to normal, if possible, before facing the sheriff.

Her left hand had many slightly bleeding, small cuts but the right hand was fine. The girl was strong for her size. After all of that pistol drawing and knife throwing, her wrists and elbows didn't seem to bother her too much. Maybe the girl was a natural.

"How many times did you throw the knife?"

"I lost track at about sixty times, but that was quite a while ago."

"Tomorrow you'll have your own holster and five or six knives, if we can find the right kind. I'll dull the edges with a file so you won't get so cut up. Tonight, get some Bag Balm from Ma Sullivan and rub it on both of your hands, but keep it off of your right thumb. You can save some for that right thumb tomorrow evening because it will be sore. I could teach you this stuff faster if your hands could take it."

Riding back toward town he asked her

how many times she had stuck the knife in the tree. She said that she didn't remember but that toward the last she stuck it four times in a row on three different occasions, and once she got five in a row.

"Missing the tree entirely is what slowed me down cause then I'd have to look for the knife. Perhaps tomorrow we'll find a little bigger tree."

Another thing seemed to help. I pretended that I was throwing at those two Bastards that raped me. I think I threw harder and that may have speeded up the spin. At any rate, I know it was harder to pull the knife out."

That evening, they ate like wolves during the evening meal at Ma Sullivan's table because they'd only had a piece of fruit the girl got from Ma the night before.

Cheyenne told Ma Sullivan they would stay several more days and she should make a big lunch for them both for tomorrow.

CHAPTER NINE

After dinner the girl stayed in their room to put the bag balm stuff on her hands and to rest.

Cheyenne went out to visit the lady of the night before, who was very good at making the town seem tolerable. Cheyenne liked the way she laughed and the fun she seemed to have. She was a bubbly lass in more ways than one, which was appropriate because her real name was Bubbles.

Bubbles was a redhead with good teeth and a bright smile, big tits and several highly developed skills. She had asked Cheyenne to come back soon, like tomorrow.

He was thinking of that now as he walked into the saloon. The place was quiet. He ordered a drink and waited to see if she would appear. The bartender asked if he'd heard the news that was going around town and Cheyenne just shook his head as he concentrated on his drink.

"It seemed that the nasty little man that

ran the greasy eatery next door may have served one too many food poisoning meals cause some unknown assailant slapped the Hell out him last night. According to the sheriff, the man had no idea who did it."

"That a fact?" Cheyenne said, as he turned around so as to keep his hands away from the bartender's eyes. He walked to a table where he could see the door and sat down. The whiskey tasted good.

Cowhands began to straggle in until there were perhaps a dozen or so, mostly locals. Cheyenne finished his drink and left.

He walked Main Street to see who sold knives and ammo. He found the General Store and luckily it was still open. Apparently the owner was about to close because he had already taken off his apron and was at the door. As he opened his mouth, Cheyenne eye-balled him into silence, put his hand against the storekeeper's chest, and gently but insistently pushed him back into his store.

"This will only take a minute, store keeper."

The man thought Cheyenne Williams to be about the saltiest looking western man that he had ever seen, which he was.

"Yes, sir. What can I do for you?"

"Knives."

"Knives, sir?"

"Knives."

Cheyenne plowed past the man to hunt on his own and found them about where he expected them to be near the gun section. He picked out the only suitable four that were exactly alike and hefted one, then threw it in a flash across the store and stuck it dead center in the neck of a store mannequin that was wearing the latest thing in ladies hats. The hat fell to the floor but the mannequin's head was stuck, pinned to the wall. The store owner was speechless.

"I'll take them all. They are gifts for my nephews."

He went across the room to recover the knife. The store man was now bowing and scraping and apparently afraid for his life.

"I want a dozen boxes of .44 ammo and a light weight holster with a small belt and a small file," then after a pause, "for my niece."

"Yes, sir."

He paid and left.

The storekeeper thought, wow, that must be some family. I'm glad they are not my neighbors.

//////////////

It was still early evening so he took the

stuff back to his room. He showed the girl her new knives and then sat down to file the edges dull so they wouldn't cut her hands when she was practicing throwing them.

She tried on the holster and they had to punch some more holes in the belt because of her small waist. She still had the empty Remington .44 so she tried the gun on for size and hefted the pistol several times. Cheyenne showed her how to tie the holster to her leg. He tied the bottom end of the holster to her shapely thigh. She was still wearing his big baggy shirt with the sleeves rolled up, the holster and nothing else. He thought her to be as cute as a button. This was the third or fourth time that he noticed what shapely legs she had.

He looked at her hands again. They were both sore but they worked. Now he showed her how to slowly draw the pistol and at the same time pull the hammer back with her thumb. Then, as the barrel comes up, she was to simply point and pull the trigger. He had her do that a few times.

"You can practice as long as your hands work, but remember no bullets until I think you are ready. When we start to shoot remember to bring wool or cotton for earplugs. You stay in and practice. I'm going out for a while."

CHAPTER TEN

He returned to the saloon and found Bubbles having difficulty with a cowhand who was insisting that she go upstairs with him. The cowhand was very roughly pulling her by the arm. Other people in the bar were beginning to notice the ruckus, but as yet no one had done anything to help the lady. True, she was a dance hall girl, but western men usually treated any woman with respect because there were so few of them. But somehow this was different; the people seemed to be afraid of this ugly fellow.

He was such a slob, that in the past Bubbles had always refused him. He was unwashed, had ugly teeth, and a nasty disposition. A moment later he was still unwashed, had fewer teeth, and no disposition.

Cheyenne Williams had hit him with a left and then conked him on the head with a pistol barrel to put his lights out. The man dropped to the floor like a sack of rocks. There seemed to be a short circuit in his brainpan because even though he was out cold, his feet were kicking a spastic rhythm against the rough pine flooring of the saloon.

"That's the best Jake has looked in years," one man said. Others smiled, pleased with the picture.

Cheyenne was very attentive as he ushered Miss Bubbles upstairs to her very feminine boudoir for a little care and feeding. The question was whose care and whose feeding. When they came down they were both wearing big dumb grins and they both looked very well cared for.

As Cheyenne was leaving, a man said to him, "Mister, you have opened a pack of trouble for yourself. That fellow's name is Jake Paterson and he and his brother are two of the meanest men in these parts except for maybe their old man."

CHAPTER ELEVEN

When Cheyenne returned to his room in Ma Sullivan's, he found the girl sleeping on the floor, so being a sensible man, he slept in the bed. When he awoke in the morning she was in there with him. Not only that, she had her face against his chest and one superb leg draped across his legs. When she moved that close he assumed in his dream-like state that is was Bubbles looking for some action, but she smelled different. He could feel himself starting to respond when he noticed there was none of the cheap perfume smell. This was all soft and fresh. When he opened his eyes he found the Kitten still wearing his big shirt. It was rolled up around her waist, and she was fast asleep.

Surprisingly enough to him, he found the situation to be a very pleasant experience. If the girl were any closer to him she would have been on the other side. In sleep she looked like a beautiful child. He suddenly felt very, very protective of her and again wondered at his own emotions regarding this girl.

As for her, subconsciously she felt very safe for the first time in many months, and was. The way Cheyenne was feeling about her, she was likely to be safe for a good long time if he had anything to say about. He was twenty-seven years old and already feeling very paternal toward this little "Kitten."

She woke up to feel him stroking her long beautiful hair. She was pleased. She didn't want him to stop so she faked being asleep until he said, "Kitten, its gun and knives time." She purred and stretched and languished all over him.

Whoops, he thought. He knew well enough that Indian girls grow up fast. He gave her pretty behind a swat and said, "Up with you girl. You have work to do."

She scowled with disappointment.

/////////////

They shopped together as soon as the stores opened; clothes and a horse for her, and whiskey for him. The Kitten got a dandy sorrel gelding that Cheyenne had traded for. When she saw it, she just beamed. Then he bought her some riding gear. When they went back to the room for her to change, she put on a shirt and pants like a man, but she sure didn't look like a man. She was far too provocative. To tone down her raging sex appeal, Williams cut the sleeves of one his shirts so she would have hands and asked her to wear his shirt over her own outfit. She didn't understand but went along with the idea. The girl apparently had no idea that she was as lush and beautiful as she really was.

He told her that most of the time she would be wearing lots of clothes and that she should get used to having these cumbersome garments on, yet still be able to find her pistol and her knives. There was some truth to that, of course.

A shade premature, perhaps, thought Cheyenne as she had yet to put a bullet in her pistol and one of the safest places to be in the entire west was wherever she was throwing those knives. There was the possibility of course of a ricochet blade sticking someone, but Williams believed that to be remote. Just the same, he did make a mental note to have his nap further away today from where she practiced yesterday.

Cheyenne was thinking, now that most of the Kitten's woman stuff was covered, he could concentrate on the real world and he wouldn't have to buck every randy cowhand in the country.

Armed to the teeth, they both rode out

of town on their mission—the girl's independence. A noble cause indeed. He was going to get her so well trained that he could just sit back and watch her take care of herself. He was having fun with the whole idea, she was having fun with the practical concept of the skills and they were both enjoying each other's company.

They had both been loners for far too long and rejoiced in their companionship. Sometimes he didn't talk to her for hours as she practiced while he napped. When he awoke, there she was working at the things he suggested she practice.

The days went by faster than he knew. One day he discovered that she was very skillful with both the knife and the draw. She could hit a target at distance with the knife nine out of ten times, and she could already cock the hammer and draw the pistol faster than the average man.

"You've come far, Kitten, but you are not ready yet.

It's time for real bullets."

The girl beamed.

CHAPTER TWELVE

"Hear me good, Kitten. With real bullets there's a good chance that you will blow off your knee cap, so for starters I'm going to put a pad under your holster that props it back a bit. If you do shoot one into the ground it should miss your foot and your leg.

"OK, start slow and draw and fire at the same tree you've been throwing knives at. Like knife throwing, you must will the bullet into a spot."

He scratched a six-inch spot on the side of the tree with his big knife.

"Watch me."

The noise startled her. It was over before she was ready and she had to get set a second time. This time she did see the movement, but it was a blur. She beamed. She thought to move that big heavy pistol that fast was absolutely phenomenal. Cheyenne didn't tell her that he had practically drawn and fired in slow motion.

By this time the girl's hands were toughening and she was very skillful at getting the hammer back. When she fired a round into the ground and the bullet twanged off some rocks, Cheyenne opened one eye from his customary nap and glared at her, decided to move further away and to have a big log between them for his protection.

He did that and went back to sleep; otherwise, things went very well, much better than he might have expected.

She was wearing fleece wool in her ears but after a time she needed the silence. They both did. Even though he had removed himself some considerable distance he didn't dare wear earplugs. He was always on his guard for trouble.

Learning to shoot was expensive but behind all of this ammo consumption was the comforting thought that there was always more gold if she needed it.

Cheyenne slept or lazed through these days of her practice sessions and he worked nights on Bubbles.

He worked with Kitten on a daily basis and for himself occasionally. He called it, "Staying sharp."

He practiced knife throwing for a half-hour and he would shoot for ten or fifteen minutes.

The girl did both about six hours a day.

She took a break every hour and lunchtime was a pleasant picnic for each of them. They found a warm stream where they could swim on hot days and from then on had all of their practice sessions near the stream.

Cheyenne liked to see the girl in the buff and once was awakened by a shot, to see her wearing just a gun belt and nothing else. He observed that this was probably the best job he ever had.

They would quit each day because her ears were ringing.

The girl reached the point where a bullet went within eight inches of where she intended at thirty feet. She could draw and fire in one smooth motion now.

It was time to start working on speed. She worked without bullets again, but she still cocked the hammer and pulled the trigger. She'd quit when her thumb, which was taped and sore, gave out.

Then she practiced the knife. She was throwing with both hands now and sticking it almost every time. She seemed to have a natural bent for the knife. At least she was quick to learn it and she no longer thought the handgun heavy. She even fired a rifle a few times.

One-day Cheyenne said to her, "From now on you are to carry two knives and your side gun all of the time, even when you sleep, until the gun becomes a part of you. You load five bullets with the thong on the hammer, and the hammer is on an empty chamber. You have one knife on your gun belt, left side, and one knife hidden. I've made this flat sheath from elk hide for you.

"The type of clothes you wear will determine where you wear your knives and the size of the knife you choose. If you wear a skirt you could strap a knife to your inner thigh but if you wear long pants you could never get to it.

"You can't ride with a knife there either. So give some thought to where on your body you can wear it. If you wear loose collars, down your back is a good place.

"Remember, your knife must be handy. So handy, you don't have to think about it. When you need it, it just appears in your hand. Once you decide where to conceal it you must practice getting it out fast.

"Kitten, your life depends on it. There's just your skill, between you and the 'man with the scythe.'

"Death is always close by, waiting to take you to the other side.

"Believe me, I know. It's been too close sometimes. Just my skill and luck has kept me around this long. Remember this. In this world, no matter how good you are, it's not good enough. You need all of your skill, Lady Luck and the Great Spirit on your side just to stay alive, even if you don't have any enemies. If you have enemies, it's even more difficult to stay alive and it helps sometimes if you can get angry."

Cheyenne Williams knew that for the girl to stand tall, look the world square in the eye, and know that she was her own master, would take some getting used too. It would all take discipline, commitment, and just plain guts. To use these weapons in her own defense was quite different from simply practicing on trees.

She was good with her skills but not yet great. She needed more time and practice. They had been at it a little over six weeks now, and both were very pleased with her progress. Williams purposely kept the girl away from town to avoid confrontation and things went along rather quietly for him as well. A month and a half was a long time for him to stay in one place and not have trouble.

He didn't want the girl to go through life terrorizing the populace the way he did. He didn't think it seemly. He would have to come up with a plan that discouraged trouble for the girl before it got started.

Cheyenne

CHAPTER THIRTEEN

The next morning they were walking to the store for supplies when two cowhands with snarly attitudes and hangovers made a crack about Indians as they passed and one of them pushed the girl.

The next thing he knew he was backed against the wall with both hands in the air because the girl was holding a knife at his throat. Cheyenne had the other one on the ground with the same result. He took their guns from them and let them go.

It was over so fast, and Cheyenne thought luckily no one saw what happened and he didn't think the two cowhands would tell anyone. It would be tough to explain how they lost their guns to Indians, especially when one was a girl.

They got their equipment and left for the practice area as quickly as possible.

The Kitten was growing claws.

They both had a good laugh on the way.

Cheyenne thought to himself, nothing

like a big long knife to give a girl confidence.

/////////////

Cheyenne was getting restless and he figured it was nearing time to hit the road. Further west. Perhaps as far as the Rockies. He had decided to take the girl with him because Turkey Flats was such a sorry place.

The way he saw it, the town had no future and there was certainly nothing here for his "protégé." The town, in Cheyenne's estimation, not only didn't have a future, it also had a dubious present. It was a hard scrabble town that raised rocks and discontent, the kind of place that was quickly forgotten and the sooner the better. The only beauty around the area was what nature provided, and there was little enough of that. What beauty there was, was not appreciated by most of the locals.

There was some unfinished business with the Paterson brothers but that was all, and if that didn't materialize, then he might just have to burn down their house, barn, outbuildings, shoot their stock, stomp the old man for raising such rotten children and cut the throat of their dog. Well, maybe not their stock and their dog. The critters were not responsible for the bad behavior of their owners.

When he thought of those boys raping his little Kitten, he could really build up a full head of steam.

He decided to bring things to a head. He set up his vigil in the saloon after one of his early visits with Bubbles.

Things fell into place for him when one of the Paterson brothers said he wanted to visit Bubbles his own self and he was not about to be put off, especially by no Indian.

Bubbles usually refused the man's attention and the fact that she preferred an Indian to him was like a burr under his saddle.

Apparently, the locals were kidding him because Bubbles preferred an Indian to a Paterson. Most people understood, once they had a look at Cheyenne Williams as compared to either of the skuzzy Paterson brothers.

Well, this was one Paterson who took scalps and he passed the word around town that he intended to do just that.

The man came roaring in looking for a cigar store Indian and found Cheyenne sitting there at a table as calm as you please.

"My name's Paterson," he said, looking at the only man in the room that he didn't know that happened to be Cheyenne Williams.

The name apparently had no effect on the stranger. Paterson was uneasy.

"Are you the Indian that's been seeing my girl?"

"Don't you have a brother that's as ugly as you are?" asked Cheyenne, still seated.

Paterson was even more uneasy. This wasn't going right. The man was still calm as could be.

Where the hell were Jake and Sam? Paterson wondered. They were supposed to be right behind me.

The batwing doors to the saloon swung open and there stood ugly Jake Paterson with fewer front teeth and his slimy side-kick, Sam. The three of them were about as raunchy a group as Cheyenne had ever seen. According to local legend they were supposed to be first class pistoleros.

The saloon citizens began to ease on out of the place before the shooting started, only there wasn't any shooting.

Cheyenne got up from his chair and said, "You men raped my sister."

Later an eyewitness described it. When Jake Paterson went for his gun, Williams hands flashed, left, right, left. He'd put a knife in the guts of each man from across the room. Then he calmly walked to them, took their guns and one by one turned the knife slowly to disembowel each man. All were still alive as he slowly retrieved each blade and wiped it across their faces. Then Cheyenne carved the letter W on the chest of each of them, stood up and announced to the room, "These men are rapists. They deserve to die slowly."

Many in the room suspected it was true.

That's how they died, slowly and in great pain.

Cheyenne Williams and the girl left town moments later leaving no trail for anyone to follow. Who would want to?

That night, all of the Paterson ranch buildings burned to the ground and old man Paterson's gun hand was shattered forever by a .44 bullet that just came out of the dark.

As Cheyenne and the Kitten rode away. Cheyenne missed Bubbles already.

Cheyenne

CHAPTER FOURTEEN

A few days later Cheyenne felt the need for supplies. They chanced upon a settlement where he was able to trade the guns from the three men for two more horses. He already had a good saddle horse for Kitten and now he outfitted his two packhorses. He bought some extra gear, food and a rain slicker for Kitten and more ammo so the girl could shoot up a storm. Then they vanished through the trees. They rode miles of stream bed to leave no tracks, and Cheyenne stopped many times to see if anyone was on his back trail.

They lazed along this way, through the hill country following westward streams where possible, for several weeks. She practiced and hunted along the way and at the same time he taught her to use a bow and arrows.

Cheyenne discovered that the girl was also a very good cook as she prepared foods from both the white and Indian world. For the first time in a long while, the Kitten was out in the world of nature once again and she was happy, content and safe. She was reminded of the days when she traveled and lived freely with her parents. This life suited her right down to the ground.

Cheyenne was happy and content and confused. He was changing.

As the girl's skills increased so did her confidence in herself. She was maturing as a woman and also as a war machine. Cheyenne still thought of her as a child but she vowed to change that. She knew about his trips to the settlements for "supplies" and she intended to change that as well one day.

/////////////

They followed a wooded stream for some miles, stopped, lunched and were having a siesta by a large pool where the river turned south. It was a beautiful warm day and they were in an idyllic setting. The horses, now unsaddled and grazing, were the sentries for the two travelers. The girl thought life couldn't get better than this. Different maybe, but not better.

She was continually reminded of how she had lived with her parents when they were alive. Cheyenne called it living the Indian way, only cleaner. There were none of the loathsome sights and smells of too many people and animals living close together.

At least the Indians bathed occasionally and moved their villages often, but the white men, except for Cheyenne, as far as she knew, never bathed and they didn't move their villages.

The girl was revolted by her uncle's world. She had never seen an outhouse until then. But she knew Ma Sullivan's house to be bright and cheery and the food smells were wonderful. Perhaps she should adapt to the best of both worlds. The White man's equipment was better in some ways and the Indian way of being close to nature seemed to her a far better way to live. She liked being where she could hear the birds sing, the horses munching grass and the sound of water in the stream falling over rocks. She liked the sound of the wind rattling the leaves of the aspen and cottonwood trees. She remembered Cheyenne calling that sound "Cottonwood music." It was a phrase he'd picked up from the father of a friend of his.

At any rate, here she was living in Paradise while just two months ago she was rolling in the dirt and miserable. She was grateful to Cheyenne and decided to tell him so when he woke from his nap. In the meantime she was going swimming.

The water was just cool enough to be refreshing and the pool was deep enough to dive in. She went into the water with hardly any splash and let the lazy current carry her down stream under water.

She was simply enjoying the sunlight on the bottom and the few fish she saw. She thought she would drift along for a while and then walk back. When she finally got out of the water, she realized it was going to be difficult walking that far on her bare feet.

Naked as the day she was born she was picking her way back along the stream when she came to a dirty camp. She could smell it before she saw it. The two rawhiders that were there didn't see her.

They were a very rough looking pair. Kitten eased back to the stream and crossed to the other side. She got into the trees and ran all the way back to warn Cheyenne. Instead of being grateful, he scolded her for wandering off without her usual armament. He was becoming increasingly concerned for her welfare.

"When you swim you take a couple of knives with you. Where are your clothes?"

"Just here by the river."

When she was dressed and armed he said, "Let's have a look at your feet."

They were bleeding, but the scratches were only minor.

The horse's ears went up and Cheyenne grabbed the girl and dived behind a big cottonwood.

Twang.

A bullet ricocheted off the tree just inches from their heads.

Cheyenne reasoned one of the rawhiders must have stumbled on her tracks and followed her here. He would have to show her how to be more careful. There was no point in getting away if you were just leading your enemies to your camp.

"You keep an eye on that fellow. Shoot if he gets too close. I'm going to Injun up on the other one and see if I can't put his lights out."

The girl said there were just two Rawhiders but there could be more. Some might just be away for a day or two. These ragtag groups were often the lowest forms of life in the west. They were here because there was no law. They found the pickings easier than working. They preyed on the helpless, raped and pillaged when they got the chance, and generally created mayhem wherever they went. They were scoundrels one and all. They were nothing new to Cheyenne Williams. He had dealt with them in one form or another all of his life. First as a victim and later as an avenger.

Rawhiders came in all colors. They were in a large way, responsible for Cheyenne handing out his kind of justice. He arrived too late to help on a couple of occasions. What he saw was etched in his memory: mutilated children, raped girls and women, the men shot and even scalped by white men to put blame on the Indians. In those particular cases, horses were left behind, but an Indian would never do that.

Cheyenne Williams championed the weak, often without even knowing it. He had planted many a Rawhider because they had attacked him and he inadvertently helped many other people by destroying these lowlifes. Their days of predation were over when they ran into Cheyenne Williams.

Now here he was at it again. Oh, well, another chancy day in this western Paradise.

This clown shot at him and he had to go. Even more important he had shot at the Kitten, which in the view of our hero was a very serious mistake, a major crime, and a capital offense. But then where Cheyenne Williams was concerned nearly everything against him was a capital offense and the bad guys always paid with their lives. Some quick, some slowly, but they always paid.

He found the second Rawhider and staked him out for the ants. He cut the man's skin every six inches from head to toe to bate the ants and stuffed a rag in his mouth to keep him quiet. Unless he was rescued, the raw hide ties would hold till the ants and the critters cleaned his bones. If the man was lucky, he would be dead before the vultures showed up but Cheyenne wouldn't have bet on it.

The dumb slob never knew what happened. He was sneaking up on the girl and then he was staked out. He didn't even know what kind of Indian did this to him and he never found out.

Now Cheyenne came up behind the man who fired the rifle. He smiled. The whole thing was a joke. He thought nobody was that inept. Yet there he was.

He found the man with a bullet between his eyes, the back of his head gone and he was wearing three knives in his brisket. The girl was vomiting her guts out. Cheyenne broke into laughter.

This girl would do to ride the river with. He was beginning to think he liked her lots, which reminded him about "supplies."

"It's time to go to the settlements for "supplies." Having said that, he smiled.

Kitten frowned.

Cheyenne

CHAPTER FIFTEEN

Some days later they came across a small band of Souix. They were a returning hunting party and the Kitten was a shirttail cousin to a captured but happy woman who had married a minor chief. It was greetings all around and an exchange of gifts. Cheyenne traded a horse for a lodge and some other goodies and set up shop. Fall was coming on and he planned to put the finishing touches to his "War Machine" and move on in the spring. He discovered the Kitten to be very good at the duties of a squaw. She could put up a lodge as well and as fast as any of the women. She settled her squabbles with the other squaws by throwing a knife into the arm of one of the troublemakers and peace was restored immediately. Even the braves who saw the incident were impressed. From then on the squaws were as docile as lambs. The Kitten was learning the value of her skill with the knife. Cheyenne was right. Perhaps she could be her own person.

She vowed to continue her practice with all of her weapons. She would practice in private away from the camp. She would leave camp on the pretext she would hunt with Cheyenne and instead, practice her weapons. She didn't want the Sioux to know the extent of her skill, so she rode great distances from the camp. More families joined their band and gradually she was riding at least three miles for privacy to practice with her weapons. It was on one of these outings that she discovered a Shoshone raiding party that was about to attack her camp. The Shoshone were painted for war and they were looking for women and horses. They certainly found one.

Little Kitten shouted the alarm as she rode right through the line of mounted warriors. She threw two knives and shot four braves before she was out of range. She killed six men and the Shoshone were so surprised at her strong medicine that they withdrew. They rode away carrying their dead.

The Sioux were equally stunned and they did not pursue their enemies, which was most unusual. Instead of counting coup on the enemy, the braves filed by to touch one of their own, the "Little Kitten" with such dangerous claws. They wanted some of her magic power.

She and Cheyenne rode out to look for her knives. They found them on a log. There was a Shoshone Lance in the ground marking a feathered shrine that displayed the two knives that held such powerful medicine that a squaw could kill from distance. The shrine was a mark of very great respect from one warrior to another. She left the scalps intact and the Shoshone were sure she did that to allow the dead to cross over to the spirit world and join the star people, the same way "Wims" would have. The Shoshone suspected that she must be Wims' woman and she was sure of it. In fact everyone was sure of it except Cheyenne Williams. So far the thought never entered his mind.

From that day on Little Kitten was known among the Sioux as "Two Knives." She was getting a reputation of her own. Cheyenne was delighted and they celebrated. They both had a few drinks, a fine elk meat dinner and later for dessert he had a luscious, ripe, and very willing, Sioux squaw.

The Kitten sulked.

Things were quiet after the usual celebratory praising, dancing, and feasting. Cheyenne and Two Knives settled in to the quiet routine daily life of the plains Indians. For a time they hunted buffalo together. Her horse didn't want to get too close to the big brutes at first, but in time it became used to the noise of shooting and the smell of blood. It was good training for them both. When they had enough robes for themselves for the winter, they traded the extra meat and robes for the other things they would need.

It was an idyllic life for Cheyenne. He lazed around with the other bucks and the girl did all of the work. They were with a larger group now and Cheyenne insisted they locate up wind and at the edge of the village. There was as many as sixty lodges now and more coming. All of the people were busy getting ready for the long winter.

It was soon obvious to the people that Cheyenne treated the girl as though she were his daughter rather than his woman. The next thing Cheyenne knew, young men were starting to bring gifts to Two Knives who by this time was a confident, comely lass. In fact, she was one of the prettiest Indian girls anyone had ever seen.

She was not the same girl Cheyenne rescued from the dirt and degradation of her skinflint uncle. Now she was happy and laughed a lot. She had a very bright smile, pretty gray eyes, long, soft, wavy, dark hair, which she wore pulled back off of her face and held with two white bone combs, one on each side. The main section of her hair flowed down her back like a dark waterfall.

The girl was lovely. She continually made and wore garlands of wild flowers in her hair. She looked like a princess and in a way she was. She was the ward of the great warrior, Wims.

In the village with the Sioux, she wore some of the nicer Indian clothes. Short deer hide skirts had a tendency to wrap around her lush contours and show off her beautiful legs. Cheyenne put her to wearing his big shirts over all of the sexy Indian clothes. He also made it plain around the village that no young men were to call on his Two Knives. At the same time he was more than friendly with many of the village's single women. He even hunted meat for some of the more attractive widows.

Cheyenne

CHAPTER SIXTEEN

One morning the village was attacked by a large Arapaho war party. The Sioux dog soldier sentries were taken out one at a time and the Sioux camp was caught completely be surprise. Many of the Sioux warriors were killed as they came from their lodges.

The Arapaho were surprised to find .44 bullets coming their way, each one taking out an Arapaho warrior. Many of them had heard of "Wims" the great warrior with the strong medicine but they didn't know they would face him on this day. Nor did they know they would face a girl warrior with nearly an equal medicine. Between the two of them, there were sixteen dead and the battle was just getting started.

In other parts of the village the Sioux were not doing so well. Many women and children were killed, lodges burned, and possessions scattered. The dead and wounded were everywhere.

An Arapaho chief saw Cheyenne Williams and Two Knives fighting side by side. There was beginning to be a pile of bodies in front of their lodge. When their knives were used up they took up their pistols until they were empty. Even the extra cylinders were empty and now they were using rifles. The chief called off his warriors because he thought Cheyenne's medicine too strong for his braves. It was a good thing for the Sioux he did, because the Arapaho could have won. Instead the Arapaho left as quickly as they had come, taking very few scalps and no horses.

The amount of destruction was incredible for so short a battle. Arrows wounded many of the people and lances wounded others. Some had their skulls crushed by war clubs. Among the warriors, the mayhem was about equal on both sides.

The new widows were cutting off a finger or slicing a breast while others were mutilating themselves in other ways. Many were covering themselves with ashes. All were wailing, trilling or singing death songs. Some of the women now had no husband, no home, and no possessions. With no one to hunt for them and no lodge, they would die of hunger in the cold of winter. It was the Indian way.

Neither of the breeds lived easy with the

idea and Cheyenne certainly didn't want this to be the future of the Kitten. He thought he might show her the good life in the white man's world. Perhaps even cut her in on some of the gold to give her financial backing.

His own thought process brought him up short. He was beginning to think more and more about the security of the girl. She really wasn't his, yet here he was thinking of her future. To even consider sharing some of his gold with her told him something about himself. He was committed to her whether he liked it or not. Perhaps they'd traveled in the wrong direction. Maybe he should have taken her east, but then, he didn't know her yet, nor had he taught her any survival skills. She was an entirely different person today from the girl he first met. She was much more of a woman now and he took a quiet pride in what she had achieved.

For now, they were planning to winter with this particular band of the Sioux nation and they would need some trade goods. A trip was planed to the nearest settlement. They would travel down out of the timber and meadow country to the prairie. The trip was to take about two weeks.

They left early the next morning. They traveled at a leisurely pace along a stream through the cottonwoods, willows and some pine. There was still plenty of grass for the horses. The autumn colors on the trees danced in the wind and the Canadian geese honked overhead on there way south. The trip was pleasant enough. Ice formed on the edges of the stream in early morning, but by mid-day it was warm. At sundown they camped in wind protected places and lazed around drinking coffee while the horses grazed. Cheyenne thought this to be a happy time with the Kitten close by and the "Cottonwood Music" playing. Cottonwood music was really the sound of the stream water splashing over the rocks and the wind in the cottonwood leaves. He thought the sounds appropriately named. Until he met the Kitten, he hadn't really paid that much attention to the beauty of nature's sounds.

They arrived at the trading post and found several Indian lodges set up there. All types but mostly peaceful.

Most of them knew of Wims by reputation and they also knew of the battle with the Arapaho. Wims was big medicine.

Some of the Indians came to pay their respects and others just to stare or to touch him. When he finally worked his way to the trading store, the word was out and even the whites knew of his exploits during the battle. They too, treated him and his woman with great respect.

The two sat in the trader's bar drinking whiskey. Cheyenne drinking slowly and the Kitten barely sipping hers but liking the warm feeling as it went down. It was warm by the big stove and they were content. Their packhorses were loaded and they were about to pull out for the Sioux village. They'd bought better knives for the Kitten and enough ammo to blow up half of the west. They purchased a rifle for the chief who led the band they would winter with.

They were quite pleased with their trade goods. The Kitten was looking foreword to getting back. Cheyenne played some cards and won a few dollars.

Making a mental note of their winter inventory, Cheyenne was pleased to see that they were well set up for the coming cold. They had plenty of buffalo robes, a good lodge, plenty of food and ammo. Their clothes were better than the usual Indian stuff. In short they were prepared for winter. All they had to do was get this stuff back to the village.

Cheyenne didn't say anything to the Kitten, but he suspected they were being watched by two men that appeared to be Buffalo hunters. They were the first of a new industry that was to reduce the vast herds and forever change life in the west.

The only thing Cheyenne had that these men might want was the Kitten. Likely, they were after her. They would bear watching.

When Cheyenne and the girl rode out he noticed the two men were still eyeing his protégé. They were seated on the top rail of a corral wrapped in their huge buffalo robes looking very like two vultures. If those two showed up he would shoot them out of the sky.

The Kitten noticed the two men as well, but didn't say anything. She had seen the look in their eyes before. She vowed to be on her guard and "sharp."

CHAPTER SEVENTEEN

On the trail once again, life was great. Cheyenne and the Kitten talked more all of the time. She was full of questions and he had most of the answers. She still practiced her knife throwing diligently. By now, she could hit a playing card at twenty feet about eight out of ten times and when she missed the card, she was still close. She rarely failed to stick the knife after she established the distance, but that was the hard part. To stick it on the first throw was the greatest challenge and that is what she was working on now. Each throw was to a target at a different distance from the previous throw. She was not only making progress; she was getting sharp. They were both pleased.

Her practice shooting would have to be held off for now. Cheyenne didn't want to give away their location. They had ridden a circuitous route through streambeds and over hard rock to make it difficult for the two "vultures" to track them.

They stayed to cover as much as possible but as they went west the country was beginning to open up. More grass and less cover except in the draws. They were in one of these many draws now. They'd camped where there was good cover along a stream and Cheyenne was listening to his "Cottonwood Music." He was having a whiskey, while the Kitten was lacerating a ten-inch spot on the side of a tree, from twenty feet away, with her many knives.

Cheyenne was enjoying watching her movements. Now she rarely missed when knife throwing, but he recalled the days when she missed often and he watched her pretty round back side as she bent over to pick up her knives. The Kitten had rounded out some since those days. He was beginning to have a variety of confused feelings about the girl. He realized he was possessive of her, but she seemed to enjoy it. He was having the faintest beginning of jealousy, an emotion that was entirely foreign to him and one he did not freely understand.

In a Crow village she might be married by now. In the whiteman's world, she would at least have one or two young lads wanting to take her to a church social. Here in the camp he was contented and even pleased to have her around. He realized he was not this contented when traveling alone. What's more, he was not likely to be ever again. This was an entirely new revelation. An emotion he would give some serious thought to. Except when he needed "supplies," he felt as though he could go on like this forever.

He taught her to shoot and throw knives so she could take care of herself. Now that she could, he was surprised to find that he wanted to take care of her more than ever.

Just before sundown he saddled his horse to scout their back trail. He rode in a large half circle but found nothing. When he returned, he picketed the horses a little further from the camp than usual to act as guards. They were placed on the only exposed side of the camp area. Then he strung a long twine about a foot above the ground from one twig to another until it blocked the open side to the camp entirely. Next, he suspended their tin coffee cups from the string and placed a few pebbles in each one. Hopefully, these would rattle an alarm if any one tried to approach during the night. It was simple but effective.

There were no takers that night. The next night after carefully choosing another defensible campsite, Cheyenne again set up the alarm system. He hoped there would be no takers, but even if there weren't, it would serve as a lesson for the girl.

However, on this night someone rattled the pebbles at the same time as the horses nickered. Cheyenne and the girl were both instantly awakened. There was enough moon to see the moving shadows. There were two shapes advancing toward them. When the shapes got close they had to cross a small open moonlit meadow.

They were not the expected buffalo hunters, but two Indians. They were both shot four times with the heavy .44's.

The girl shot as skillfully as Cheyenne. Each person, making sure to protect the other one. When they looked around the horses were still picketed and Cheyenne assumed rightly that if there were more Indians around, they would have tried to take the horses. When he said "tried," he meant just that because the big Appaloosa wouldn't go anywhere, except for Cheyenne Williams. He would be more likely to take someone's head off.

Cheyenne dragged the bodies out of the camp area and left them for the critters to feed upon. From the look of them the next morning, they appeared to be the equivalent of the white man's rawhiders. They were a sorry pair. Scrounging a living the easy way, without pride, village or tribe. They were probably outcasts from a tribe a long way off. Cheyenne knew all of the tribes in this territory and these men were from none of them.

Late afternoon of the next day saw them safely back in their lodge among the Sioux. They felt the temperature dropping as they arrived and were glad to be back. That night it turned very cold and the following morning the village was greeted by a howling snowstorm.

There was enough dry fuel for a few days so they stayed inside under their robes and were as snug as bugs. Their tipi was insulated by air between the two layers of hides. Snow piled up around the base acted as additional insulation against the cold and helped to keep them nice and warm. Even at these temperatures, it was sometimes necessary to open the smoke hole a little further to cool off the tipi. Cheyenne had his whiskey and he watched the girl cheerfully do all the work. From his point of view, it was the perfect way to sit out a storm, or even the entire winter.

Cheyenne

CHAPTER EIGHTEEN

Cheyenne managed to take on "supplies" one afternoon when the girl was out seeing to the horses. He was beckoned to the nearby lodge of a dark eyed beauty who was recently widowed during the battle with the Arapaho. Fortunately for this young widow, she was being fed and cared for by her brother.

Cheyenne had hunted meat for her some time back and she was hunting meat from him now. She wanted to be grateful. Apparently several of these dark eyed damsels found it convenient to be grateful during these severe snowstorms.

Some dusky damsels were grateful throughout the entire winter and some were even grateful all year around. Cheyenne preferred this type and looked foreword to being a recipient of their gratitude through the long, dark winter. The winter was long but it wasn't all that dark. It only seemed so because he was deep between the buffalo robes with a dusky maiden and didn't see the bright sunshine on a many a bright wintry day. He was too busy racking up quite a score.

The Indians rarely made war during winter. It was a good time to restore the soul. Cheyenne figured he had a lot of soul restoration to do, assuming he had one, of course. He was willing to work on that, providing he could get these dark-eyed beauties to give aid, sustenance and comfort. The temptations were so numerous that his soul was repaired in no time, while his body was nearly torn in half.

To make matters worse, the Kitten was becoming more and more of a tease. He could see that it was going to be a long winter. No wonder people called the Indian men, braves. Cheyenne found new meaning for the word, "brave." He smiled to himself knowing full well that he had never had it so good.

Cheyenne Williams further endeared himself to the tribe by hunting meat for these same pretty widows. He figured it was the charitable thing to do. After all, there was more than one kind of hunger. Since the battle, some of the women had remarried or moved in with family. Others became the second or even the third wife to a warrior. Cheyenne did not take a wife because he knew that come spring he and the Kitten would head back to the whiteman's world.

Cheyenne owned several good horses, which he acquired by gambling with the other braves, or in gunfights, by shooting their owners who would no longer need them.

At the moment he was riding his favorite Appaloosa and leading three packhorses loaded with meat and their camp stuff. The temperature was never above freezing so the meat stayed frozen. The meat they would consume each day was carried in a leather pouch against the side of the girl's horse. The animal's heat kept those small pieces thawed out for their next meal.

They'd been away two days on a hunting expedition, which was very successful. Game was plentiful. The Kitten was skinning out their most recent kill, a big young bull elk, while Cheyenne napped under warm buffalo robes. He thought the trip necessary to rest up from the rigors of village life, and she thought the elk hide would make a beautiful and very short, seductive dress to charm Cheyenne.

The Kitten realized she had a lot of very stiff competition, but she felt she was up to the challenge. So did everyone in the village except Cheyenne. He was still thinking of her as the girl child and still called her "girl" more often than he called her Kitten. She was becoming a woman right before his eyes, yet he seemed reluctant to admit it even to himself.

During the coldest days, Kitten worked the elk leather to make the white, sexy, two-piece dress to dazzle Cheyenne. She sewed beadwork on the bleached white leather. She cut a fringe at the bottom of the short wrap around skirt.

Kitten periodically sewed and wore the skirt to perfect the fit. She always did this when he was there and she modeled the skirt for him without wearing anything over her magnificent breasts. Then she said, through her bright innocent smile, absurd things like, "Do you like it this way or should it be tighter?"

She was so provocative that Cheyenne could have chewed nails. He marveled at her beauty and went looking for "supplies."

The kitten was beginning to get the attention of Cheyenne Williams. Living this close to such a provocative child was beginning to get on Cheyenne's nerves. As he still considered her to be a child, and in a way she was, and still his ward, she was most definitely a "no-no."

CHAPTER NINETEEN

For peace of mind, he went on a long trip alone. He first made sure the chief would keep an eye on his Kitten and that she was well supplied with meat and other foods.

The girl was very disappointed that she wasn't to go along. Williams assumed and rightly that it was still winter and the village wasn't likely to be attacked until spring, if then.

Cheyenne camped alone for the first time in months and rather enjoyed it for a few days, much to his surprise. He had traveled alone most of his life and fell into doing for himself as though there never had been a Kitten to make camp and cook for him. It was still winter but the cold was not severe. The signs said that early spring was not far off. There were buds on the willows and their stems had taken on the purple color that comes before they leaf out. The ice along the streams was melting by mid day only to harden up again at night.

Some of the larger beaver ponds were ice free near their intake streams. Cheyenne saw signs where the beaver had checked over and repaired their dams. There was very little snow at this time so traveling was easy. He fed mostly on small game. He carried pemmican and whisky. What more did an outdoor man need?

After a few weeks he felt it was time for company. He rode to a white settlement that was called Jackson's Hole. The place was situated at the south end of a valley and up against some steep hills.

The "Hole" was a world of white due to a recent snowstorm. It was surrounded by snow-covered meadows and pine forests backed by beautiful, majestic mountains that seemed to reach the sky. These were the Teton Mountains, named so by the French trappers because they resembled a woman's breasts.

It was a difficult trip through the mountains. The temperature dropped rapidly after the storm. Deep snowdrifts and severe cold would have turned back a lesser man, but Cheyenne was determined. He plodded on, driven by his confused thoughts that, for the most part, involved the Kitten. He felt she was infringing on his freedom. He assumed if he was away from her for awhile, perhaps he might get back to his selfish, non-caring, normal self.

Jackson's Hole wasn't much, but there he found warm shelter, whiskey, a few tired whores and a card game. He availed himself of everything except the whores. They were a sorry bunch.

The log buildings were built heavy against the hostile Indians and the weather. He was able to buy ammunition and a few foodstuffs that made the trail more pleasant, such as coffee, bacon, flour, beans and whiskey. With the price of beaver down, the "hole" was populated by hordes of disgruntled mountain men. Most of them were sure the price would come back, and a few others were equally sure the good days were over. Many were planning to hunt buffalo, come spring.

Cheyenne Williams seemed to fit right in with these fellows. He had spent some time trapping several years ago and more recently he'd done a little buffalo hunting. He didn't like trapping as it was hard work, and cold hands and feet went with the territory, and he didn't like buffalo hunting on principle. He thought just taking the hides was a dreadful waste, which it was, and shooting the poor dumb brutes, diabolical. At the time, there were so many that no one thought they would ever disappear, including Cheyenne, He was just against the slaughter and waste on moral grounds.

Since that time he'd found gold and no longer needed to work. Becoming financially secure changed Cheyenne's philosophy of life in a very great way. Since finding gold, he had time to think, to read, and to go where and when he pleased. He always had very good equipment and the best horses. Life was good. Well, it still was, but the Kitten had certainly managed to start his head spinning.

After being in Jackson for a week, he was asked if he cared to go along with two men to the Salmon River country. Just to have a look.

He said, "Why not."

They left the next morning. The names of the two mountain men were Tiny and Doc. Both names were misleading. Tiny was a giant of a man and Doc was an abbreviation for Dociene.

Doc had patched a few gun and knife wounds but he was certainly no doctor. Both men had traveled together for a very long time and they were extremely capable.

As often happens, men seem to team up with partners that can make a contribution to their work and their life. These two complemented each other in many ways. Tiny had strength and power and Doc was a small man who was unusually cheerful. He also seemed to have most of the brains. Tiny was misleading in that he often deferred to Doc's judgment, even though his own brain-pan worked well enough. They were a good team.

They had simply wanted Cheyenne along because he was likable. Of course they had never seen him angry. There weren't many men alive who had.

The men traveled together and got acquainted around the evening campfires. They all liked being free and this was a life that was about as free as life could get.

Most days the sun was out and they were safely camped against the cold by sundown. Their packhorses carried an ample supply of warm Buffalo robes and they had plenty of food.

They slept on and under the heavy buffalo robes with their heads covered, and when the snow fell, it just helped to insulate them against the cold. When the winds blew they stayed in camp. It was slow going some days because of the deep snowdrifts, but no one cared. They found a hot spring that wasn't too sulfurous and stopped for two days to enjoy a bath. They sat with guns near, neck deep in the super warm pool, wearing their hats, sipping whiskey during a snowfall.

They traveled through mountains and valleys—so pristine that they looked as though they had been made just the day before. Cheyenne suggested that the area was so perfect that its design must have been a team effort by both the Indian Great Spirit and the Christian God. The men looked across vast panoramas of untouched wilderness. In some areas they were the first white men to see this country. The air was very still in the bright sunlight and nothing moved. The snow had driven the critters down lower and game was scarce.

Some days later they traveled west of the Yellowstone through the Shoshone country without seeing any Indians and felt lucky to have kept their hair. Even Doc, who was bald as an egg, had been very nervous.

They camped for a few days at the base of the Boulder Mountains where there were great elk herds wintering on the willow shoots that grew near the beaver ponds. They ate elk till it came out their ears and then trout until they were tired of that, and finally moved on up over Galena summit, which was about nine thousand feet high. The air was thin and the terrain steep. It was necessary to rest the horses often. Finally they descended into the Salmon River country.

The headwaters of the Salmon River began as a ditch a foot wide. The river, situated in a huge bowl between mountain ranges, began as run off from the Saw Tooth Mountains. Later it flowed into the Snake River and then into the mighty Columbia that flowed all the way to the Pacific Ocean. In late summer, the Salmon that spawned in the headwaters of the Salmon River had to travel a thousand miles from the ocean to get back to where they were born. It was one of the longest migrations of any fresh-water fish.

In this great bowl, the three men set up a more permanent campsite. Here they waited for spring. They were catching a few salmon, which was a wonderful treat. Spring came late this high up. Each man had time to rest up the horses and repair his gear.

One day Tiny returned to camp with a small deer and reported seeing many tracks from unshod horses, about a mile from their camp. He couldn't tell if it was a hunting party or a war party. The men would go lightly until they were sure.

Cheyenne said, "You fellas stay put and I'll track them. I might be gone a few days."

Cheyenne found the pony tracks and followed them, not the way they were going but back the way they had come. He followed until dark, made a cold camp and followed them again the next day. He was sure they weren't a hunting party. They had passed up much game and there was no sign of anyone skinning out an animal carcass. Still, they could be just travelers, but that wasn't likely this time of year. The snow was still deep in places this high up.

Cheyenne discovered the tracks led to a trapper's cabin. He found two scalped trappers. One was mutilated and the other was nearly dead.

"Who did this to you?"

He had to repeat the question. Then the man's eyes opened. He wanted water. Cheyenne gave him some and then the man said in a raspy voice, "Renegades, more'n a dozen. We didn't have a chance."

He started to point the way they went but died before he could finish the gesture.

Cheyenne looked in the cabin and found a third person also dead. He was a boy about twelve or thirteen years old. He too had been mutilated. There was nothing of value left in the cabin. The renegades had taken everything.

Cheyenne pulled the two dead men inside the cabin and then poured coal oil around inside and touched a match to it. He rode away without looking back.

CHAPTER TWENTY

Cheyenne Williams was angry. He was going renegade hunting. He put on an all white doeskin outfit, checked all of his weapons, and loaded all of his extra cylinders. He got out his short bow and the half dozen arrows he used to hunt silently. Now he was wearing two six guns, carrying four knives, and his bow and arrows. This way he could sometimes get two or three deer at a stand where as with a rifle, the first shot scared the rest of them away.

He rode back along their tracks until he came upon the group in early afternoon of the second day. They were a small group of Blackfeet renegades, the equivalent of western bandits. Some had whiteman's clothes and two had rifles. One loud mouth had a six gun in his belt. He was practicing his quick draw. He didn't seem to have a holster or any more ammunition than was in the gun.

Cheyenne tied his horse far back from

their camp and waited till dusk. He wanted as many of them as possible to be around their campfire. After watching their camp for some time, he was able to determine that there were fifteen men in all.

One man was just coming into the camp when Cheyenne intercepted him, putting his huge knife in the man's throat from about twenty-five feet away. The man died silently, in seconds. Cheyenne recovered his knife and covered the man with snow.

Next he shot three arrows at three men who all died within seconds of each other. The other men scrambled for cover. He managed to kill four more with his knives, all silently. He had yet to make a sound and the remaining men were really spooked at this quiet death. They were so confused that they actually shot one of their own men. The poor fellow was gut shot with a rifle bullet. He was one of the two men with a rifle. Both the rifles the renegades were using were old muzzleloaders.

Cheyenne didn't give anyone a chance to reload. It was gun time and Cheyenne Williams promptly shot the remaining men as fast as he could fire. With the speed of a ghost, he ran swiftly from place to place firing at them as he went. He dropped renegades like a scythe does wheat.

Miraculously, even though an arrow scratched him, he was not seriously hurt.

He took no scalps. That and the four knife wounds told anyone who discovered the bodies that "Wims," the great Cheyenne warrior, killed these men.

He recovered his knives after carving a "W" on the chest of three of the dead. He then tied all of the horses head to tail and led them out loaded with all of the gear and equipment of value.

Later, two Blackfeet warriors found the bodies. The legend of "Wims" was enhanced once again.

The renegades were left to the critters, which is what they deserved.

Cheyenne returned to the camp of the two trappers, Tiny and Doc. That night he drank whiskey with them and said his farewells. Early the next morning Cheyenne Williams left to return to the Sioux village and the Kitten. He was smiling with anticipation. He had been away almost two months.

Cheyenne

CHAPTER TWENTY-ONE

When Cheyenne returned to the village he was greeted warmly by the tribe, and especially so by the Kitten. He learned the Kitten had been involved in an altercation with one of the squaws.

Apparently, the squaw was rebuked by a less than ardent suitor who preferred pursuing the Kitten. The angry lady, finding no fault with her own charms, assumed the Kitten had deliberately set out to steal her man, and went after the Kitten with a knife.

The Kitten, who was totally unaware of the would be suitor or the outraged Indian lady, suddenly saw an angry Indian squaw running at her with a knife, screaming her name, and threatening to kill her. She reacted by throwing one of her knives fifteen feet directly into the woman's chest. The woman died immediately. Many of the village women were witnesses to these events and the Sioux nation suddenly had greater respect for the knife throwing skill of the

Kitten.

The Kitten's claws were getting longer. As the attempt on her life was witnessed by several of the villagers, she was not blamed and the matter was dropped.

////////////

The dead woman had relatives and Cheyenne decided to leave the Sioux village immediately. Cheyenne, who by now owned twenty- two horses, gave two horses to the parents of the dead woman and eight horses to the village chief whose name was Blue Feather. Blue Feather agreed to look after the remaining horses for Cheyenne until such time as he might return. In the meantime, the chief could use them as his own. Cheyenne and the Kitten rode out of the Sioux village the next day leading two packhorses.

CHAPTER TWENTY-TWO

The two riders headed southwest at a leisurely pace. The weather was still cold but the days were bright and sunny. It was now late winter and spring was beginning to show more positive signs. The snowmelt in the afternoon lasted longer and the willow tips were showing a brighter purple above the snow along the streams and run off areas. The ice was melting on the beaver ponds and a few beaver were seen occasionally, making repairs on their dams or cutting willows for food.

As the travelers moved further southwest the country opened up from meadow and pine forests to prairie and fewer pines. There were usually many cottonwoods and willows in the draws. As they traveled they passed over a wide ocean of grass and undulating hills. Antelope dotted the landscape everywhere and some were so curious they came within fifty yards of the two riders. They passed buffalo and other edible critters, but saw nothing of hostile Indians.

Wherever possible, they followed streams leading westward and left them when they turned north or south.

Sometimes they were the highest beings on a vast flat sea of grass, from horizon to horizon. Domed by the great sky, they simply followed the sun. At night they camped and watched for shooting stars. The rare snowfall barely covered the ground and did not impede their progress.

One day they shot two buffalo and stayed in camp for a few days to skin and process the hides. The meat added to their meager larder. Life was good. They were warm in their small traveling tipi at night and they had good buffalo robes to wear when they traveled. They were both happy until they met about twenty ragged-assed Arapaho who were on the verge of starving. They were on the move because they had hunted out the game where they were.

The Arapaho Indians recognized "Wims" and were afraid to come near him because of his strong medicine. When he made the peace sign, they still would not come. He had to send the girl to parlay with them because apparently a few of their warriors were in the battle with the Sioux and had witnessed his devastating destruction. It seemed none of them were aware that the Kitten was also in that battle.

Cheyenne shouted to them that he was leaving food for them. He gave them three dressed out sections of one of the buffalo he had shot and wished them well. He did not honor them with the best parts of the buffalo such as the tongue, the liver, or the hump roast.

The meat was laid on the ground for the Arapaho; then he and the Kitten rode off.

The Arapaho were more confused than ever by an enemy who would kill them one day and leave them food the next.

Cheyenne

CHAPTER TWENTY-THREE

Cheyenne Williams didn't tell Kitten, but he and the girl were gradually making their way to his gold stash. He was running low on spending money. They wanted to go west anyway and they could easily swing by what he called his "Golden Place." It wasn't far and it wasn't out of the way. The gold lay mostly in the roots of an old fallen cottonwood. All he had to do to get the gold was pick it out of the tree roots and then throw dirt over the roots again until next time. It was necessary to cover their tracks well to ensure the glory hole was not discovered by anyone else.

When they were within a half day's ride of the gold, Cheyenne decided that the Kitten, for her own good, should not know where the gold was. It was in a very rough area indeed. This was very rough country and if anyone even had a vague idea where the gold was, they still couldn't find it. They would have to know exactly where to ride in and then exactly where to look for his gold.

Cheyenne had found it quite by accident. He had crawled into these rocks to avoid a harsh, cold wind during a severe winter blizzard. He had found a well-protected place near a stream and put up a lean-to in order to get out of the weather. He put it next to a huge, old and fallen cottonwood tree. He'd placed buffalo robes over his pole frame and built a small fire. It was just dark when he finished.

He was snug in his camp, making coffee, when he noticed several bright yellow reflections of the fire, dancing at him from different places in the tree's roots. When he crawled over to investigate he discovered that they were gold nuggets. Some were bigger than a thumbnail. He picked up about a hundred of these nuggets and then he dug down through the surface dirt where the tree had been and found many more, some even larger. Cheyenne carefully replaced the dirt in the hole and cleaned out all of the gold in the tree root that was above the ground. He camped one more day by his glory hole and decided not to file a claim but rather to keep the place a secret. He'd been living off of those nuggets ever since. This was his third trip back to the site.

When he had all of the gold he needed,

he rode back to the girl and then they continued on toward California. It was a long way, but they had plenty of time. They traveled at a leisurely pace, hunted occasionally, and watched the world come out of winter and emerge into spring as the days became warmer.

////////////

They rode down out of the high country to the nearly flat prairies in time to join a wagon train that was headed for California. The people were unhappy with the idea of half-breeds joining up with the train but the wagon master, who's name was Kinkaid, knew of Cheyenne Williams by reputation and wanted him along as a scout and perhaps a hunter. He said they would need the extra guns in case of an Indian attack, which was a very real possibility.

They rode by day and camped out under the stars by night. They traveled with the wagon train but a little apart from them. Where possible, Cheyenne camped in concealed areas or where he had some forting-up capability, in case of Indian attack. He was relying on his Appaloosa stallion to act as guard dog and warn him if anyone was snooping around, and one night it happened.

Cheyenne

Two young men from the wagon train were bent on mischief. They had seen the Kitten several times around the evening campfires and thought her the best looking girl in the wagon train, which she was.

They believed she would be honored to accept their charms, what with her being an Indian and them being white and them being closer in age than that old man she was traveling with.

It happened that on this particular evening about dusk, the Kitten was at her campsite alone, and Cheyenne Williams was talking with Kinkaid about the scouting job. The camp was about a hundred yards from the circled wagon train and the two young men had sneaked away when they saw Cheyenne talking with Kinkaid.

The two men arrived at the campsite to find the Kitten trying on her new white doeskin dress. It was the one with the short skirt that showed off her beautiful legs and her marvelous derriere. The girl heard them before she saw them and assumed that it was Cheyenne returning. When she looked up she could see this was not a friendly visit. The men had split up and were circling around to get her between them.

The Kitten realized her weapons were a few feet away except for the throwing knife that hung down her back.

The men were grinning like wolves over meat. In an evil way, it was exactly that.

Thinking her to be defenseless. One of them said, "You're going to enjoy this, squaw."

She could read the lust on their faces and it reminded her of the two brothers back in her uncle's hotel. She had vowed then that such a thing would never happen to her again, even if she had to take her own life. Now, thanks to Cheyenne Williams, she was a very different person. Now, by God, she had claws and was perfectly willing to use them. She would take their lives if necessary.

"You two fellows leave this instant. Go on, get out. "I'm warning you."

After seeing the Kitten in her provocative short skirt, the sap was really running in those boys and they were not about to leave until they had pleasured themselves.

When the men got within twenty feet and showed no sign of going away, Kitten showed them her knife and they just leered. One of them said, "Be careful you don't cut yourself, at least until after we have finished with you. Then we might do it for you."

The two men had actually discussed sharing her all the way to California if she was cooperative and raping and killing her if she wasn't.

Kitten threw her knife into the guts of the man closest to her. Then rushed for her weapons and was about to shoot the other man, who was drawing his gun, when the big Appaloosa stallion trumpeted a scream and put both of his front feet against the man's chest as he ran over him. In addition to knocking the man down, the stallion took a big bite out of the man's neck on the way by, which was probably lethal. The wound was gushing blood. The horse turned on a dime, reared and trampled the man to death. The girl was astonished by the fury of the big horse. By the time the girl calmed the horse, the man's corpse was pulp.

Cheyenne heard the screaming horse and came on the run, followed by Kinkaid, to find the Kitten hugging the big horse and crying.

Cheyenne was not surprised to find that his horse had killed a man but he was surprised to learn the horse obviously accepted the Kitten into the family and was protective of her much like a trained guard dog.

Cheyenne made sure the Kitten was all right, then went to the man with the knife in his guts, who was still alive, pulled out the knife, and said, "Tell me what you're doing here before I skin you alive." He then, immediately cut the man's chest from his collarbone to the knife wound inflicted by the girl.

The man screamed in pain.

Kinkaid was objecting to this treatment of the would-be rapist. Cheyenne gave Kinkaid a vicious look and Kinkaid withered. Kinkaid knew he had just looked Death in the eye.

Cheyenne placed his big knife just under the man's skin and began to cut slowly, the man fainted. Williams revived the man with cold water, threatened to do it again and the man told the whole story. Kinkaid listened and later told the people on the wagon train.

The man died a slow and agonizing death. He was still alive in the morning, but only long enough to see the shovels, when Kinkaid came with a burial detail. When those men saw and smelled the gut wound on this man and what the horse had done to the other one, they vomited.

Minutes after the confession of the dying man, Cheyenne and the girl moved their camp and left Kinkaid to clean up the mess.

Later, Cheyenne went with Kinkaid to the wagon train and asked if either of the dead men had family with the train. The two men were traveling with the wagons but neither of them had any family with the wagon train. The pilgrims on the wagon train thought Cheyenne was inquiring about the men's family because of remorse or sorrow. The pilgrims couldn't have been more wrong. In fact, he didn't like loose ends, and would have killed anyone who was related to either of those two men or anyone who might have been a threat to the girl.

Kinkaid later told a friend that the two dead men were lucky to have died as quickly as they did because he was sure that Cheyenne Williams would have designed a much more terrible and slower way for them to die, which was true.

Cheyenne was glad he had trained the girl so well, but he was perturbed because she was not fully armed at the time.

He vowed to teach her a new mantra. "Fully armed at all times. Fully armed at all times."

CHAPTER TWENTY-FOUR

The wagon train pilgrims were learning that the further west they rolled, the more bark there was on these western citizens.

It was a few more days down the trail when Kinkaid, the wagon master, rode up to Cheyenne Williams to ask him if he would scout ahead of the wagon train instead of just hunting meat for them.

The killing of the two men had made it difficult to convince the wagon people that Williams was the right man for the job. When Kinkaid finally convinced them, Williams refused.

Cheyenne didn't need the job or the money and he certainly didn't want to leave the Kitten alone, especially if Kinkaid had a train full of any more riffraff. The discussion went back and forth until it was finally agreed that the Kitten would go wherever Cheyenne went.

When told of this turn of events, the Kitten beamed. Cheyenne and the girl would be gone a few days at a time, There job was to find the best trail and the best water and grass for the wagon train and its stock.

Kinkaid was very pleased. There was no one better to spot Indian signs or to parlay with them if it became necessary.

It did become necessary and Cheyenne did parlay with them, all two hundred of them. They were Shoshone Indians on their way to the high country for the hot season. They made this annual trek to the mountains to get out of the heat of the prairies and to get new lodge poles for their tipis. It was always a frolic for the Indians on this trip and they couldn't have been friendlier.

Chief Black Horse led these Shoshone Indians. He was a wise old man of many summers. He knew of "Wims" and welcomed him to his fireside to smoke the pipe. Wims could talk the language and the chief wanted to know how many white men there were.

"As many as the grasses of the prairies," Cheyenne answered.

"Do they all have fire sticks?"

"Yes, if they want them."

"Where do they go?

"Most go to Oregon and some to California."

Chief Black Horse had heard of Oregon but knew nothing of California. Cheyenne said, "It is as far as the great water."

The Chief recalled having heard of that place.

Cheyenne was asked if he thought the white man was a threat to the Indian's way of life?

"Some will stay here," he answered, and nodded his head. Most will pass on through the Shoshone country.

"White men will not be a problem for some time yet. Perhaps one day, they will be a problem for the Shoshone."

Chief Black Horse knew of the mountain men who came to his land for beaver and he knew the wagon trains increased in number each year and didn't like it. He wondered what would stop them from coming. There was already talk of the Chiefs getting together to decide what to do about the white man. This was most unusual because some of the tribes had been at war with each other for generations and now there was talk of putting their differences aside to deal with the white man. The word was that some of the eastern tribes were being pushed from their lands. Sometimes just for the land and sometimes for the shiny metal.

Cheyenne left the Chief, having exchanged presents and swearing friendship and peace between them, no matter the fu-

ture difficulty between white
man and Indian.

At his suggestion the wagon train had continued on while he palavered with the Shoshone.

When Cheyenne caught up with them it was the next day, as he was to spend the night in the lodge of Chief Black Horse. He was offered a very willing woman who was rather attractive and had her own lodge. She was also part of the Shoshone hospitality. The lucky maiden was only one of many who had volunteered for the task. It seems that Cheyenne Williams was very handsome to all women.

When Cheyenne left the Shoshone woman he gave her a present and promised to see her again. At the time, he really meant it. The woman beamed.

When he caught up to the wagon train the next day, he was whistling to himself, and the Kitten, who had been left behind, was very perturbed.

CHAPTER TWENTY-FIVE

Scouting for the wagon train was turning into work and Cheyenne Williams was about to tell Kinkaid to get someone else when the train was struck by an Assinaboin war party.

A warrior named Bright Star, who was trying to make a name for himself and become a chief among his people, led the war party. He had been causing much grief to the few wagon trains that had crossed through that part of the country. But then, the Assiniboin were known for causing grief to any one other than themselves, and even to each other, on occasion.

The wagon train was hit while Cheyenne and the Kitten were scouting ahead. Luckily, they were close enough to hear the gun shots and raced back to the train to see Kinkaid trying to turn the wagons into a circle. When Cheyenne and the girl rode into the closing circle they were given supporting fire. They each shot several Assiniboin warriors on the way in and the Kitten received a deep cut from the edge of a passing arrowhead.

Once inside the wagon circle, they helped hold off the attack. The fact that they each shot so many Indians endeared them to the people on the wagon train and there was no more complaining about the fact that they were half-breeds.

The Kitten showed that she could shoot. Cheyenne was still the teacher. He taught her to lead her rifle on a running target. She caught on quickly and was soon shooting as well as any of the pilgrims even though this was her first battle with Indians and her first real use of the Winchester rifle.

Cheyenne had heard of this young buck that was so bent on killing. During the height of the battle, he yelled his war cry and a challenge to Bright Star. All of the other Indians heard the challenge, but Bright Star refused to accept the challenge.

The Indians were riding around the circled wagon train as they attacked, and they tried to get close enough to jump their horses over the barricades. Each time they attempted to get close they ran into withering fire and left many dead warriors and wounded horses in front of the barricades.

Cheyenne told Kinkaid to have his

people shoot the Indian's horses. There were two reasons for this: first, the horses were easier targets and second, an Indian afoot was less apt to penetrate the circled wagon train fortress.

The Assiniboin weren't the horsemen that the Cheyenne Indians were, but they could ride well enough. Many of them would slide down on the off side of their horse so as to make as small a target as possible. They did this by hanging on with just an arm and a leg and by putting their foot through a strap that went around the horse's belly. They barely peeked over their horse's shoulder all the while riding at full speed. They would ride close and shoot a couple of arrows and then ride away again. There was very little target for the whites to shoot at until Cheyenne and Kinkaid told the whites to shoot the horses. Once the horses were down, it was much easier to shoot their Indian riders. There was very little cover for them to hide behind on the prairies.

Bright Star found a low barricade and decided to rush that spot. He called for ten of his warriors to follow him. Cheyenne heard part of this command and guessed the rest. When Bright Star charged the barricade, he ran into a devastating fire from Cheyenne and the Kitten. Bright Star and his warriors were shot to pieces. The last two charging Assiniboin were killed with thrown knives. Cheyenne shouted to the attackers in their own language that he, Wims, had killed Bright Star and the remaining Assiniboin rode off.

They knew Wims medicine to be very strong and none of the remaining attackers wanted to go against him.

Bright Star was supposed to have great medicine and when Cheyenne killed him, the legend of Wims was further enhanced. From then on, there would be fewer attackers once it was known that Wims led the wagon train.

Braves that were in this battle and lived to tell about it received much status from their people when they returned. The Assiniboin had been fighting the Cheyenne for generations, but now none of them wanted to fight Wims ever again.

The great warrior Wims left a mountainous pile of Assiniboin dead in front of the barricade Bright Star had attacked. He fired so fast that he had literally burned up his Winchester and emptied both of his handguns.

The Kitten and two or three others contributed to the devastation.

The Bright Star raid was to live in sad memory for generations. Losses of men and horses were very heavy during that raid. The villagers were to mourn for many days. None of the bravest warriors returned, and that particular band of the Assiniboin Indians did not recover.

There were wounded and dead among the wagon train people but nothing to what it might have been if Cheyenne and the Kitten were not present. The wagon people were truly grateful. Kinkaid moved them on down the trail away from the sight of the battle so they could bury their dead. They rested for only a half a day and then went on to put miles between them and the battle site.

Many miles later, when Cheyenne felt it was safer, he posted guards and the train rested for a few days. During this rest period one of the widows who was not all that fond of her husband while he was alive, decided to be grateful to Cheyenne for saving the entire wagon train from "ten thousand" screaming savages, single-handed.

He smiled.

She was young, lush, ripe and pretty and had been married to some old geezer who was killed in the attack. It was a perfect situation. Later, he was sure of it.

She was about as ripe as one can get and still be unplucked, so Cheyenne in his infinite wisdom accepted her gratitude with a specialized gratitude of his own. The problem was that the wagon train was rather a small one and even though the woman had pulled her wagon off to the side, that night every one knew what was going on in the McLaughlin wagon.

Cheyenne found he had a screaming tiger by the tail and she didn't seem to want to let go. She didn't want to let go that night, nor the next day, nor the following night. When the two of them finally looked out, the entire wagon train was no where to be seen.

Kinkaid, the wagon master, had judiciously decided to move on up the trail before there was rebellion in the camp. The wives were thoroughly outraged at the behavior of the McLaughlin woman. Some of the women were simply green with envy and so were some of the husbands.

Mrs. McLaughlin on the other hand, was wearing a big dumb grin on her face, and was sure that she had just had the best experience of her entire life. She rationalized, after all, she was just being grateful to a surviving war hero. It was practically the "Christian thing to do."

Cheyenne Williams too, was grinning. He assumed his bites and scratches would heal before he was called upon to champion another great cause. He hung around the wagon train for more gratitude and gradually drifted back to his campsite to find that the Kitten had taken her belongings and pulled out. At first he couldn't believe it. Why would she do such a thing. Then he was sure she would be back. Days later, when she hadn't returned, he was calling her an ingrate.

The Kitten had left to avoid the heartache she felt caused by Cheyenne's escapades with women. He still considered her a child. He didn't realize that she loved him. His nose was out of joint for many weeks. His wrath was formidable. Even Kinkaid was giving him a wide loop. When Cheyenne bedded the McLaughlin woman, he really put her through her paces. When they were finished, the woman was very pleased and exhausted, and Cheyenne wore a big grin for about an hour.

The woman just beamed. Everything she owned hurt, but in a nice way. She told one of her girl friends on the train that she was beginning to refer to her wagon bed as "our battlefield." She giggled and claimed that she always won. Cheyenne's sessions on the McLaughlin "battlefield" calmed him temporarily but the anger arose within a few hours and he was difficult to be around until after the next "battlefield," encounter.

He spent many hours in the company of his new lady.

In fact, he was with her whenever he wasn't scouting for the wagon train. He thought of taking her along with him the way he had the Kitten, but to his amazement, he discovered that she didn't even know how to saddle a horse and gave up on the idea. Still, she did have certain skills and Cheyenne Williams had great respect for certain types of specialization.

CHAPTER TWENTY-SIX

The Kitten was angry that Cheyenne had not come after her. She'd left a plain enough trail. Looking back on the whole thing she was disappointed. She was aware that he might like his freedom more than he liked her, or more than anything, but she didn't want to believe it.

Now she had dealt herself this hand and she must go through with it. Her pride wouldn't let her return to the wagon train, not yet, anyway. She had a good saddle horse and a fair packhorse loaded with camping stuff, lots of ammo and assorted killing equipment. She wasn't afraid to be out there alone, but she was a little uneasy. It was her first time in this vast wilderness alone.

She wished she had a dog along. She missed Cheyenne and found herself wondering what he would do under these circumstances. Where would he go? What would he watch for? How and when would he travel.

Many things from his teachings began

to come to her mind. First, her Mantra came to mind, "Always go armed." Cheyenne would always watch his back trail. Who was sneaking up on him? He would be on the look out for game. If he shot something, then he would move on for several miles before skinning the critter. These thoughts running through her mind gave her a sense of closeness to Cheyenne and a sense of confidence in herself.

This was her first night alone on the trail. She looked for a place well hidden and easily defended. She wisely decided to have a cold camp and no fire. She wasn't the coffee enthusiast that Cheyenne was, and therefore didn't really need a fire. Then, over the next few days, she was careful to leave as little evidence as to where she was going as possible. She rode the streambeds where she could and the hard rock on occasion. However, she was quite certain an excellent tracker such as Cheyenne could follow her, but few others. There were other predators in this wild country besides animals, and she didn't want to be surprised.

She was riding west, enjoying the new sense of freedom and her rising confidence. The weather was warming, the country was not as flat as it had been and the grass was greening up. The migrating birds were returning north and insects were flying about.

She managed to catch two fat trout using insects for bait on a hand held fish line. She missed Cheyenne's company very much, but otherwise she was doing very well.

The Kitten had seen no one but she did see plenty of game, and her skills with a bow were adequate enough so she was well fed. She judged herself to be many miles south of the wagon train, yet going in the same direction and at about the same speed.

Late one afternoon, she came across a wolf pup caught in an Indian snare. The pup had found his supper caught in the snare and in the process of killing the rabbit had got himself caught in an adjacent snare. The pup was caught by a rawhide loop around his right back foot. He was hanging from a sapling, upside down, and squealing his lungs out.

The Kitten was careful to see that there were no other wolves around and then she put her gloves on and cut the critter down. She held onto the branch that the rawhide thong was tied to. The wolf pup was still caught by the thong so she could place some water and food near him. The pup drank and ate as though he had been hanging from the sapling for a year instead of a day or two. That meant that whoever had set these same snares would be back soon to check on his catch.

The girl threw a big robe over the pup and tied the ends closed. Then she put him on her horse and rode out of there at a canter. She pondered the growling lump in front of her and thought to herself, "Now that I have the critter, what am I to do with it?" The horse didn't like the idea of carrying a wolf pup and the pup didn't like the rocky ride. He wasn't into personal abuse and he certainly didn't like his bouncing carpet prison. He was very indignant. He squealed and growled and was generally obnoxious until the Kitten reached inside the robe and swatted his backside. He yelped and was quiet. Later he got motion sickness from the movement of the horse and barfed all over the inside of his jail. The Kitten washed the robe in the creek and dunked the pup several times until the assorted horribles were more or less out of his fur. After that treatment he was sure he hated her.

She made an early camp that day. She made a collar and extended his tether so the pup could run around a little. He was only pint sized but he had needle sharp teeth and he bit her. Again she swatted his backside and he was learning to dislike this lady a whole lot. He yelped for the second time and was sure these tall vertical human types were into all kinds of abuse. He vowed to escape as soon as possible once he figured out how to do that.

The pup was lying down, feeling sorry for himself and watching her every move when suddenly the woman brought him more water and food. The Kitten had shot a doe with a bow and arrow earlier that morning and had not yet skinned it out. Cheyenne had taught her to hunt quietly so as not to give away her position and at the same time scare away the other critters she might desire to hunt the next day. She chose this time to do the skinning job, and while doing that she tossed bloody scraps to the pup. He was in "pooch heaven." The food was great and he didn't have to scrounge for it. Perhaps the woman was not so bad after all.

The pup was so full he was ready to burst, for neither of them really knew how much he could eat. He had never had the chance to find out and she hadn't fed dogs in many years. The pup must have been weaned early because he did right well on a raw meat diet for such a little guy. He romped and played and chewed on every thing until she gave him small bone scraps to gnaw upon. With that discovery they were both happier.

The pup helped the Kitten keep her mind off Cheyenne and the pup was beginning to imprint on the nice lady who fed him. He had long since chewed through the rawhide thong that he had been tied with.

He escaped and was joyously frolicking around in the pine forest when he became hungry and there was no lady to feed him. He looked for food for two days and finally gave up and retraced his steps, only to discover his benefactor had gone. He followed her scent for another whole day, and when he caught up to her, he was all in.

He was a fat little puppy when he left and now his bones were showing. He was just too small to hunt for himself. He had managed to catch and eat a mouse during his three days in the wilderness.

When the nice lady fed him again, he was very glad to be back.

The Kitten missed the little fellow when she noticed that he had chewed his way to freedom. She didn't give him much of a chance of surviving alone. When the wolf pup returned, she was overjoyed.

She said to him, "Little puppy, you look out for me and I'll look out for you," and she handed him another piece of meat.

When the pup's belly was full, he seemed to be smiling.

"It's about time we gave you a name. If you are going to be a part of this family, there are many things you must learn. One of the things is that I'm the boss and another is that there will be times when you must be very quiet."

They came to a small stream in an idyllic setting and she camped and lazed her way for several warm days. She repaired a few items the pup had damaged and alternately played with him. The little fellow had boundless energy. The pup thought this was great stuff because the nice lady didn't growl and bite back.

They both ate, slept, and swam. The swim was a surprise to Kitten. She went in the water armed with only two knives, one strapped to each thigh. This was a new visual for the pup. He wasn't used to seeing her without her clothes and at first he growled at her.

When she went in the water, he did too. It was a pleasant surprise for each of them. He didn't follow her out into the deep water, but he did swim around near shore and acted like he wanted to follow her. The water was cool and refreshing and had the effect of bathing them. In the pup's case, the water got rid of some of the horrible smells he was carrying around. Kitten just felt cleaner and it was a nice way to spend a hot afternoon. She dived down deep enough to see some large trout.

After the swim, she caught two large trout for dinner, one for each of them. The pup ate his raw but she ate hers cooked over a small flame. It smelled so good the pup wanted part of her share and she gladly gave it to him. More "pooch heaven."

Like Cheyenne, she used her horses as watchdogs. They were always hobbled or tethered near by. She still practiced her knife throwing and by now was very accurate. One day after her swim, she tried on her new white elk hide outfit, the one with the short skirt. It still fit perfectly, only now there was no Cheyenne Williams to see her in it. She diligently sewed some more beads on the garment, but her heart wasn't in the task. Somehow life with out Cheyenne just wasn't as much fun anymore.

CHAPTER TWENTY-SEVEN

A few days later it was no fun at all. Two crusty old men, who looked as though they might be trappers, captured the girl. She was playing with the puppy and had carelessly allowed them to sneak up on her. They held her at gunpoint. One held a rifle on her in front and one held a rifle on her from the back. They each spoke to her so she would realize they were in front and behind which made her virtually defenseless. They didn't come close and didn't threaten her in any way. They simply wanted her to make them some new clothes. They were "old timer" mountain men and saw her as a squaw. She was outfitted better than they were and they assumed that she was the squaw of some important Cheyenne warrior. That part was true, but not the way they thought. She did not let on that she understood their language or that she fairly bristled with knives.

They had taken her guns and assumed she was defenseless. She prepared a meal for them and then they made hand motions that implied she was to go with them. She packed her gear and headed out. The pup followed at a discrete distance. He didn't like these strangers and he was getting hungry. He was just learning to adjust to his old world, and now he was to have a new one. When Hal saw the wolf pup, he simply said, "Wah," which in mountain man language, stood for everything.

The two mountain men were both ancients with plenty of bark on them. There was still beaver but the price wasn't what it had been and one of them thought he could see the end of beaver. If that was so then it was also the end of a free way of life. The other man said beaver would go on forever. There was more beaver in these mountains than there were stars in the sky. That part was true, or nearly so, but it was the dress codes of Europe and the East that determined the price of beaver pelts. The threatening, high silk hat was just around the corner.

The name of these gruff old mountain men was Sumi. They were the Sumi brothers and they each answered to the same name. If you were talking to one, you were talking to both. They did have first names but few people knew them or even bothered to use them. Their real first names were

Harold and Keith, but they were called Hal and Keifer.

Unlike most mountain men who came west to the Shining Mountains, these two fellows traveled east to get there. They were berthed on a square-rigger that was out east in the China trade. There father was the ship's Captain and the boys grew to manhood as part of his crew. The ship received a cargo for San Francisco and when they arrived, the two young men decided to have a look at the "Shining Mountains" they had heard so much about.

They left the sea in San Francisco, strong as bulls, with enough money for good outfits, good horses and good rifles, and traveled east with a yearning to see the Mountains. They found them and never left. They had been up and down and over and around from here to there. They hunted, packed, guided, trapped, and just hung out, until one day they looked at each other and saw that they were getting old.

They were still full of mischief and though capable, they didn't have a mean bone in them. They had each planted a few men who did have a mean bone in them, and somehow they both had managed to keep their hair in all of this Indian country.

Their buckskins were almost black with

dirt, age, sweat, and wear. Hal made a sign to Kitten that he would be pleased if she would make him a new set of buckskins. She knew how but acted as though she didn't understand and the two men thought they might have captured a "real slow in the brain-pan." Keifer rolled his eyes and said, "What do we want with her in the first place?"

"She sure is nice to look at."

"She ain't ugly, I'll give you that."

"Wah, ain't ugly," Hal exclaimed. "Hoss, we've never seen better in all of our travels. Not even among those dark eyed beauties in the Sandwich Islands, was there one to equal her."

"She sure as hell beats looking at your ugly face," said, Keifer.

"Hoss, she does at that," and both men smiled.

"How are you going to get her to make us some new buckskins?"

"I don't know yet."

"We might try being nice to her." Keifer said, and he continued, "I don't understand why we haven't seen some redskins looking for her, unless she ran away from her people. We could lose some hair over this one. Do you want to keep her that bad?"

"We've risked hair over a lot less. Wah!" Hal was big on saying "Wah."

He found the word useful. It meant nearly everything from surprise to an affirmative. He even found it useful to say after he had killed a man.

The word "Wah" was a favorite with other mountain men as well. It still meant almost anything from a question to simple emphasis. Men who live alone and go without speech for months at a time often need few words. When they do have a chance to talk with someone, it is often brief.

The brothers used other mountain man expressions and Kitten was to learn a few. Such expressions as "prime beaver" meant anything that was good or beautiful. "Shines" meant the same thing.

They often referred to themselves as "this child," meaning the first person, or me or I.

The three of them were traveling west and the two men were finding her nice to have around. She talked little, did most of the work, and was very nice to look at. She even smelled good. When she had traveled with Cheyenne, she did all of the work, so in this situation she actually had it easier. She insisted on feeding the little wolf pup that followed them at a distance. At night when they were camped, she went to feed and play with him. In a few days the pup was coming into the camp in the evening to sleep near her.

Her cooking was better than the brothers, so they went for it. These two had lived entirely on meat most of their mountain lives and usually without salt. They did trade with the Indians for other foodstuffs and occasionally, at a fort or trading post, they picked up other prepared foods. They were enjoying her cooking and she was great to look at.

CHAPTER TWENTY-EIGHT

Early one afternoon, while traveling south, a small band of renegade Indians attacked the group. These motley renegades were the pirates of the mountains. Too lazy to work, they stole what they could and murdered for the rest. They wanted the six horses from the brothers plus everything of value they could get their hands on.

When they attacked they didn't know the Kitten was a woman as she was wearing a hooded coat at the time. It was a gift from Cheyenne. He got it for her when he traded several horses for some useful things, like guns, ammo, and whiskey, from Jim Bridger at his trading post.

The brothers were quick to find protective rocks to shoot from and they dropped a few renegades in short order. They could shoot. Kitten implied that she could shoot and one of them said, "Wah, but at who?" One of her knives appeared and stuck his sleeve to the log he was shooting behind. She retrieved the knife, and said, "Gun," and they just shrugged and pointed at their horses, where the guns were.

They thought if she was that good with a knife, she could have killed them any time in the last few days. They may as well give her a gun, too. The Kitten rushed to the horses, was about to be caught by a renegade Indian, when the man died in front of her with a rifle ball in his brainpan, put there by one of the brothers. She got her guns as quick as lightning and then shot two renegades as soon as she returned. The brothers just stared. One of the bad guys managed to climb the rocks to get a better shot at them and the Kitten took him out with one of her throwing knives.

The Sumi brothers were savvy old codgers, and when they didn't have a man target they shot the horses of their enemies. Put a man afoot in this country and he was most likely under. It also got the attention of the enemy. They had come to get horses, not to leave any. They were beginning to believe the people they were attacking had stronger medicine than their leader. Shortly thereafter when their leader was killed, they were sure of it, and they called off the attack. Then they high tailed it out of the area. They had lost half of their men, which numbered about nine before the attack. Now they were down to two healthy men and three wounded, one of them seriously. They were all angry. They had hoped for so much and received nothing but dead and wounded.

The brothers most certainly did have strong medicine. They had much better rifles and were more skillful at using them than the renegade Indians.

The Indians learned that if they stuck their heads up, they were shot between the eyes.

The renegades had carefully chosen the sight for the ambush, had surprise on their side, but still they were badly beaten. To stay around was to die. These men were terrible people, but they weren't stupid. They left the scene as fast as they could, two of them on foot.

The ever-resourceful Sumi brothers gathered up all of the guns and valuables, such as ammo, saddles and other tack. They managed to rope two horses that had run off and loaded them with as much stuff as they could carry, and then they all moved on, keeping a wary eye out for trouble. The old boys were crafty enough to ride the stream for several miles before they came out at a place that was solid rock. They left almost no trail.

Some days later the brothers found a

different stream in a deep draw with cottonwoods and willows and decided to camp for several days. The horses were getting too thin. There was an angular look to all of the livestock.

Keifer said, “We all look as though we've been rode hard and put away wet. I'm plum worn out.”

Even the Kitten was ready for a rest, though she was the least tired of them all.

The wolf pup was ready for a rest as well. He had taken off when the shooting started and came back when all was quiet. He smelled the dead Indians and growled. That night he stayed so close to Kitten that he touched her the whole night. He slept with his chin across her leg.

//////////////

The next morning after the sun was well up, Kitten decided what she really wanted was a bath and she took one in the river. The brothers watched and then watched some more. So did the wolf pup. Then he went in too. Finally Keifer said, “That girl shines.”

Which was a very high complement in mountain man talk. Hal agreed by saying his usual, “Wah.”

She told them in their language that they

both needed a bath. They, who had not bathed in years, both looked insulted. One of them said, "Wah." Then they looked at each other, knew the girl was right, and began to undress. Even in the water they were only two feet away from their guns so they didn't feel too vulnerable and the Kitten swam with two of her knives.

The old guys made sure they were out of the water before the girl got out. They wanted to see her in the buff as long as possible. The Kitten found that she liked their admiration so long as it remained a distance away.

The girl was getting the respect of the two men but more important, she was no longer a captive. They were not ready to treat her as an equal yet, but that was mostly because she was a "Breed."

They had every reason to believe that she was a singular fighter. She'd proven that, but they still thought the horses and the guns were theirs. They had been together too long to adjust to the concept of three equal shares, at least, not yet. The Kitten didn't complain and as long as they were going the same way she was. She knew it was safer traveling with these two than traveling by herself.

The group lazed around the camp for many days, hunting, eating and resting. There was game for them and many plant foods to eat, such as wild rice, chokecherry, rose hips, berries of many kinds, and wild onion and cattail. Life was good.

The Kitten did most of the cooking. She made several kinds of stew and roasted many kinds of meat. And the men provided game. She told them what to shoot and they brought it back to camp. The brothers ate better than they had in years. When just the two men traveled together they ate for sustenance. With the girl doing the cooking, the food was much tastier and they ate for the enjoyment of it as well as sustenance.

The Kitten knew the men were enjoying the meals because they ate everything in sight and then stretched out to snooze, belched and said, "Wah!"

These two old rascals were beginning to like their "squaw girl" more than a little bit. In fact, they had become downright fond and protective of her.

Squaw Girl, for that's what they called her, was the nearest thing either of them would ever come to having a daughter.

They had become right proud of the little lady. They frequently said things like, "She surely shines," or, "She is some," to be followed by the inevitable, "Wah."

When the Kitten swam or bathed they never missed the chance to watch, yet neither of the men ever made any rude remarks or advances toward her. The girl liked being admired for a change even by these two old duffers. She was becoming fond of them. Cheyenne, conversely, was usually trying to get her to cover up, and he rarely said anything complementary to her unless it was about her survival skills, which by now were considerable.

The Sumi brothers thought her beautiful and told her so in their own rough way. After a time, she showed them the white dress she was working on. She sewed beads and porcupine quills on the garment as color accents. It was nearly finished and it fit perfectly.

When the Kitten put it on, the two old men knew they were being privileged to see her wear it. The men were speechless. Neither of them had ever seen a more beautiful woman. After that, they treated her like a queen, with even more respect, as if she were a real lady, which she was, in a kind of natural way. They began to ask what she might like to do, or where she wanted to go, whereas before, they simply told her what to do and where to go.

The brothers became more protective of her and gradually she endeared herself to them to the extent that they felt a genuine affection for her and she for them. She was lonely without Cheyenne, and they helped fill the void for her. The brothers felt as if they had been sent a star from heaven to brighten up their lives. They didn't like the idea of going back to the days before she arrived. They had talked among themselves and hoped she wouldn't leave the group, but knew she was young and lusty. They expected her to find a man one day and each of them secretly vowed to himself to hate him immediately.

Meanwhile, they liked listening to her singing when she worked. Some of the songs were rather bawdy, which really tickled them. They also liked her sense of vitality. The girl was the picture of health and very happy with life.

She made garlands of wild flowers and wore them in her hair or around her waist. The girl even made garlands of wild flowers for the two mountain men, which they wore. They felt a little silly, but they wore them any way. They were getting to the point where they would do about anything to please Squaw Girl.

One day she went for a walk in the forest and came back into camp dressed only in maple leaves and wild flowers. The girl had used the stems of the big maple leaves to weave and hold the leaves together. Each leaf overlapped the next and the stems were punched through the leaf itself to hold the next one. The leaves went around her much like flexible shingles with each row placed over the row below. The maple leaves were large so it didn't take long to make a very short skirt. She was wearing a very short provocative skirt and a brief bodice around her breasts and in her hair she wore a maple leaf crown that she had decorated with wild flowers. As her ears were pierced, she wore wild flower earrings that were the color of magenta. On each wrist and ankle she had a bracelet of small green leaves and wild flowers. The girl looked to be a forest Goddess. The old boys were impressed and speechless. She was so beautiful. They just stood up and stared. She had really pulled their heartstrings. They knew she had dressed this way just for them and they both had tears in their eyes. Then she gave them each a hug. They were now a family. That day she named the pup "Wolf" and decided to make the two men some new buckskin clothes.

She already had the buckskin to make each of the old boys a new outfit, but she had to be tactful and not play favorites. She had them strip to the waist, and then she measured them with a rawhide thong. The system worked fine. When the shirts were done, she went through the same procedure to measure the pants. The old boys giggled and were slightly embarrassed, which seemed odd to Kitten because they had all been swimming in the buff together. But then she hadn't tried to measure the inseam of their pants before. In a week the outfits were done and they fit very well. The old boys were very happy with their new duds. In fact they were ecstatic.

Kitten planned to do a little bead work design on the shirts, but they wouldn't give up the shirts unless it was real warm, so she settled for a small design on the front of the left shoulder just below the collar bone area of each man's shirt. It was her-own special design. She was pleased and so were they.

The design was a three-inch by three-inch wolf head. Wolf sat and watched her work so often that the idea of doing his picture just sort of happened. The two men were really proud of the "picture work" and so was the Kitten.

The old boys couldn't wait to show off their new outfits but there was no one around except their own group, their horses, and doubtless a few enemies. Keifer showed his new outfit to his horse.

The critter was momentarily stunned

and a little skittish for some time. Keifer not only looked different but also he smelled different. Even the horse thought it was an improvement.

Wolf cared little for the duplicate pictures of himself, but he was sure there was something going on that he should be proud of anyway. And he was. He strutted to the excitement and was about to lift his leg on Hal and establish his territory when he received a kick that sent him away on the run. The old boys surely looked different and they were glad of it.

Cheyenne

CHAPTER TWENTY-NINE

Scouting ahead of the wagon train perhaps by ten miles, Cheyenne Williams came across a Lakota Sioux Indian with an arrow through his lung. He was trying to sing his death song when Cheyenne rode up on the big Appaloosa stallion.

The dying man told of being shot only minutes before by one of the two men he was hunting with. This was an apparent murder. Otherwise, the braves would have stayed until the man was dead and then taken his body back to his people. If enemies had shot the dying man from a different tribe, they would have taken his scalp.

Cheyenne gave the dying man water and stayed with him. Before he died, the Sioux told Cheyenne his name was Two Bears, and that he had been killed by evil men from his own tribe who's names were Small Horse and Elk Antler. Two Bears thanked Cheyenne for the water and had another drink. Moments later, Cheyenne told him, "The people call me Wims."

"I have heard of you," he said, with his eyes focusing on Cheyenne's face.

"It is an honor to die with a great warrior." Then he died.

It wasn't long until Cheyenne saw the two braves. They had stopped in a shady wash to rest their horses. They were eating pemmican and talking in low tones. The pair was too far away for Cheyenne to hear what they were saying. The standing one seemed nervous and his gestures were more animated than the other man.

Cheyenne startled the two men by shouting his war challenge to them. He had painted his face for battle. Then he shouted his name to the two men.

"I am called Wims."

They must face him in battle or be branded cowards.

One man kneeled down and began to sing his death song. The other shouted back his challenge as he leaped to his pony and charged with a lance. Cheyenne riding swiftly to the attack notched an arrow to his bow, and when he was within range sent it to the charging man's lungs, but the arrow glanced off the hard buffalo hide shield. At the last second Cheyenne swerved his horse and passed by the deadly lance as the Indian brave turned his horse to charge again. This time as the two charging horses bore down on each other, Cheyenne threw the big knife very hard. It went through the Indian's war shield as if the shield were paper and directly into the Indian's chest. The tip of the great knife stuck out of the man's back and flashed in the sun as the man fell from his horse. Cheyenne stopped by the dying man and carved a "W" on the man's chest using the tip of the warrior's own lance while the man was still alive. Cheyenne said, "Your death is traded for the life of Two Bears."

Cheyenne put his foot against the dying brave's chest and slowly pulled the huge knife from its prison. The act was done without mercy.

He thought to himself about Arthur pulling Excaliber from the stone.

The dying murderer knew nothing of King Arthur, but Cheyenne was sure if he had, he would have thought the huge knife blade to feel as long as King Arthur's sword, Excaliber. Cheyenne Williams wiped the bloody blade on the man's buckskin pants. Then he mounted and rode back to the death song singer.

Finding the brave who was still singing his death song and fully expecting Cheyenne Williams to dispatch him to the spirit world,

Cheyenne ordered him to get up. The man was stunned. In a moment he did as he was told.

"Which of you killed Two Bears?"

The terrified man simply pointed at the dying warrior. This was the same man that seemed so nervous earlier. Because of the murder, he was sure Cheyenne had been sent by the Spirit world to avenge Two Bears' death and in a way he had been. This is what the animated argument had been about as Cheyenne rode up on the two men. The surviving brave had predicted the appearance of just such an avenger because of his friend's awful deed.

Cheyenne's appearance was much sooner than expected and that was why this second man immediately began to sing his death song. He thought it pointless to fight or run. Which was true. The terrified brave was sure Cheyenne was an apparition from the Spirit World. He was dressed in his very used and darkly weathered to almost black buckskin outfit. He was wearing a wide, flat brim hat with an eagle feather tied on a short tether to the crown. The feather could always float on the wind over the wide brim. The Indians believed the feather offered prayers to the four directions and the earth and sky. In addition, this apparition he was clearly seeing was fairly bristled with weapons, whose use could only be guessed at by the terrified warrior. Cheyenne was carrying a bow, arrows, two belted Remington .44 six guns tied low, two Remington .44s as saddle guns tied at the horse's withers, a Winchester .44 rifle, a two shot .44 Derringer neatly hidden behind his elk antler belt buckle and four knives, three of which were concealed. The huge knife on his belt was the avenging weapon of Two Bears.

The warrior explained that Two Bears was killed because he refused to give his consent for his daughter to marry the other warrior even though the man had offered many horses. The daughter did not want to marry the warrior. The people could verify the fact that there had been much hatred between the dead warrior and Two Bears. The warrior added, "But then you already know that since you are from the Star People of the Spirit World." The man still believed Cheyenne to be a spirit; therefore, Cheyenne assumed he was telling the truth.

Cheyenne showed the man where to load up Two Bears' body. Williams, still mounted, looked down at the man and said, "Return to your people and live honorably. Tell them Two Bears' death has been avenged. You will take Two Bears' body with you and give him an honorable funeral that he may live eternally among the Star People. The murderer stays here to be forever tormented by the demons.

Then they each rode their separate ways, the Indian, not to the Spirit World, but to his village and a new life, and Cheyenne, to the world of spirits which really meant the wagon train. That's where the whiskey spirits were and, of course, "supplies."

CHAPTER THIRTY

Cheyenne Williams rode a slow lazy three-day ride to rejoin the wagon train. He'd found an easy route through this country where there would be plenty of water this time of year for the stock's needs. He could see the country beginning to dry out and thought it best to keep the pilgrims moving. A few weeks from now this would be very dry country indeed. He would speak to the wagon master and try to get a few more miles behind them each day. They could expect more frequent delays and breakdowns the farther west they rolled, as the country became more difficult. There would be places in the Rocky Mountains or the Sierras where they would have to lower their wagons down sheer cliffs. Here in the open grassland they were making good time, but Cheyenne felt they would have to do better if they wanted to avoid being caught by an early snow when they got to the mountains. California was still a long way off. Cheyenne would advise the wagon master to give the pilgrims a pep talk.

That evening Cheyenne Williams rode into the wagon train camp with some fresh meat that he dropped off at the McLaughlin wagon. He was greeted enthusiastically by "Mack," for that's what he called her. She was smiling from ear to ear and was holding a bottle of whiskey in each hand. Williams jumped down, picked her up high enough to bury his face in her big tits and gave her a crushing hug. The hilarity was interrupted by the arrival of Kinkaid, the wagon master.

Over whiskey, Williams drew a map in the sand as he explained the route the wagon train was to follow and where he thought were the best places to make camp each night. Kinkaid seemed satisfied and left. Cheyenne Williams returned to his "supplies." Afterward, the two of them sneaked down to the nearby stream for a refreshing swim and more "supplies."

In the morning the McLaughlin wagon pulled out along with the rest of the wagon train. It was much too dangerous to be left behind like the last time. Williams had leaned on Kinkaid and on the widow's hired helper. He told the man to be sure her wagon was ready to pull out with the group, no matter what was going on inside. If some ladies in the wagon train were embarrassed, that was their problem. "Besides," he added, "I doubt if there is a virgin over thirteen in the entire wagon train." This comment was probably true.

"This is Indian country. The McLaughlin wagon rolls with the rest of them, or else. You got that?"

He left the "or else" part up in the air, so they could imagine what he might do if it happened a second time.

Cheyenne was very irritable and he finally had to admit to himself that he missed the Kitten. He missed having her bring him his whiskey when he returned from a long scouting ride. He missed her singing and the little things she was always doing for him. He really missed watching her. She was a great to look at. She was what he called "a great visual." She was very provocative, and now that she was gone life seemed rather flat.

As he began to realize just how important she was to him, he became even more irritable. Cheyenne sulked around the wagon train for another two days, sipping whiskey until he was wound up as tight as a clock spring. By now he had worked himself into minor rage.

How could she do this to him. He was

her protector and her mentor. He still didn't realize that he was behaving like a jealous husband. He had witnessed jealousy in others many times but continued to think her simply ungrateful. Nevertheless, he was concerned for her safety and he had better get up off his ass and find her before she ended up in some warrior's tipi.

He told Kinkaid that he would have to do without him for several days, to follow the ridge until the wagon train reached the river, and then to follow that to the big canyon. He would try to meet with them there.

"Wait two days. If I don't return, you're on your own." With that he rode out, leading two packhorses.

Kinkaid had mixed emotions about seeing him go. They really needed his know-how but it was nerve racking to try to deal with a man who was as explosive as a live bomb. Kinkaid had perceived the problem all along, but had kept his own counsel. He didn't want to lose a good guide.

CHAPTER THIRTY- ONE

Cheyenne left the wagon train during a gray drizzle that did not help his spirits. He headed South, hoping to run across the tracks left by the Kitten. It was not going to be easy because he'd taught her well. If she used any of the savvy he had taught, only an expert tracker could follow her. She had time and weather working for her as well. He didn't backtrack to find where she left the wagon train, but instead headed where he hoped to intercept her. He reasoned she would ride parallel to the wagon route for a time and then, if she was doing well on her own, she might later, as fall came on, head further south for the warmer weather. He still assumed she was going to California. He didn't know it, but he had guessed right on both counts.

Williams knew the print of the Kitten's horse as well as he knew her face. If there were prints visible he would find them.

The next day the weather was much

improved. The sun came out and restored his spirits. It felt good to be on the trail again without the responsibility for Kinkaid and the pilgrims. Now, if he could just run across the Kitten. What would he say to her? Should he spank her?

He smiled at the thought of wailing on her exquisitely rounded backside. No, he didn't think so. To do that would be a sacrilege and, besides, she was no longer a child. As he thought about that, it really occurred to him for the first time that she was not a child, but in fact a young woman, a very attractive woman. She was doing the very thing he had trained her to do. She was making her way in the world on her own and answering to no one. She was her own person and she was very well prepared to defend herself if need be. This was hard country for anyone alone. He hoped she was all right. She was certainly not prepared to meet an Indian war party, but then, who was?

Cheyenne didn't like the thought of the Kitten alone in the country ahead. He knew the Indians from here on would be far more trouble than any Indians they had run into previously. He spurred the big stud to a cantor. The horse didn't care for the spurring and put his ears back. Cheyenne had been trailing at a fast walk, but now said, to the big horse, "We've got ground to cover. Let's move."

Cheyenne

BOOK TWO

THE SEARCH

Cheyenne

CHAPTER THIRTY-TWO

Assuming the girl was south of the wagon train and on a parallel route, Cheyenne was pushing the big horse at a grueling pace. After several miles he was sure he had missed her track and he had to circle back and nearly start over. The Kitten had been away several weeks by now and the trail was very cold. He assumed she was leaving signs for him to follow at first, but later on she would be much more careful to hide her tracks. She was taught to ride streambeds and to ride over hard rock when she could find it, even to drag a large tree branch to erase the horse tracks that went into her camp.

Her two horses had eight feet, plus her own footprints if she walked, meaning there could be as many as ten prints for each step. Surely, she would leave something for him to follow.

He discovered that he had taught her too well. It was easy to miss a footprint when she was trying to rub them out with a tree branch. She was thorough enough to do it twice if she felt it necessary. No prints ever led to her camp.

It was in one of these erased track areas that Cheyenne had ridden over and missed her track. When he circled back he rode a different way and finally discovered the Kitten's tracks. Now that he had found them he could hurry along and follow her.

He camped where she had camped and strangely enough, he was surprised to find he enjoyed a feeling of closeness to the girl just from being where she had been. He saw where she had built her fire and where she had slept. He read all of the camping signs. He saw where she had practiced knife throwing and was pleased to see how all of the marks in the tree were within four inches of each other. He even saw where she had entered the water for her swim. He was very much looking forward to seeing her again. He thought fondly of the carefree days that they had traveled together while she was learning her shooting and knife throwing skills.

As the days went by, he was aware that he had taught her well because he lost her trail several times and had to ride the rivers or streams several times to find where she eventually came out. The bare rock was even more difficult. When he lost the Kitten's track on the rock he had to ride the edges to see where she came out onto the softer ground. All of this back tracking cost him several days. A lesser man would not have been able to track her at all. The wind and rain were constantly rearranging her tracks until they looked like any other undisturbed surface. Ghost like, the tracks simply vanished in many places. Still, there were enough faint traces that Cheyenne knew he would find her. Finally, after some weeks, the tracks were becoming clearer. He was getting closer.

The fact that she had found the wolf pup had changed her travel pattern and she had not tried to cover as much ground each day. Either she was waiting for the puppy or he could not stand the motion of riding. Cheyenne correctly surmised the later and was grateful to the wolf pup for slowing her down.

It was a good thing that the Kitten's pace was slower. Each time he stopped to rest he asked himself if anyone was worth all of this trouble. Each time he thought of not having her in his life, he would mount up and push on. He was slowed in catching up to the girl because even his big horse was showing signs of the pace. The weight had fallen off of both of them. They simply had to take some time to rest. Now that the tracks were clearer he figured he could afford the rest time even though he was impatient to see her and to know that she was all right.

CHAPTER THIRTY-THREE

Meanwhile, the Kitten and her entourage of critters were making their way along a shallow creek bed. She was trying to make it very difficult for anyone who might be following her. She had long since given up on the idea that Cheyenne Williams would be coming along.

If she had known he was following her she would have built fires every fifty feet or even turned back to meet him half way.

She secretly hoped he might be back there somewhere trying to find her and she was aware that if he was following her, no amount of covering her tracks would stop him if he was determined to find her.

Things had gone well enough so far and she had discovered many things about herself. She was finally her own woman. She could take care of herself and her critters out in the wild world. She felt confident about her ability and felt very good about herself. She liked the way she looked, but without

Cheyenne's presence in her life, she just wasn't happy.

Each night his image came to her mind like a ghost and she often slept fitfully, waking in the morning to a mood of fatigue and melancholy. She was becoming irritable which was not her nature. The Kitten didn't like herself very well these days and she was very angry with Cheyenne. She knew he belonged with her even if he didn't and she very much resented the fact that he hadn't come after her.

If she ever saw him again she planned to tell him how she felt whether he liked it or not. If she could face up to Cheyenne Williams, and she was going to, she was a very changed woman indeed. More than she knew.

/////////////

The Kitten continued to travel along with the Sumi brothers and her wolf pup but she was beginning to suffer from a mild form of melancholy. The two mountain men noticed and were concerned. If "Squaw Girl" wasn't happy, then neither were they.

"Maybe we should all go to Mexico and see the dancing." We could hang out in the warm sun for the winter."

"We always liked it there."

"It's a long way to go just to see dancing."

"You always liked looking at those senoritas."

"That was before we found Squaw Girl. None of them will look as pretty as she does."

"Why don't we ask her what she thinks of the idea?"

And so they did.

She was still hoping that Cheyenne Williams would show up, but a few days later she reluctantly agreed to head out for Mexico. As they traveled, the Kitten felt the distance as though it was a heavy weight on her heart. She was moving farther away from Cheyenne with each step. The trip was slow, ponderous and hot. The wind whistled through these canyons with a soulful moan, one could easily imagine as being that of ghosts.

After traveling many days in the whistling wind country where the winds were about to drive them all mad, and later along the Verde River, they came to a pleasant little village called No Name. It was located on a wide shallow stream that watered the lush green trees all around. The place was an oasis. The town was laid out along the stream and had the appearance of being part of an old mission. There were two cantinas across the street from each other. They bordered the square where a rather imposing church slept quietly in the noon day sun. The village loafers, who were lolling about in the shade, were mostly Mexican.

The three travelers stopped at one of the adobe cantinas to have a store bought meal, some cheap booze and a rest. As they entered the thick walled adobe building, they were surprised to discover the room was cool and comfortable. There was a slight breeze blowing through from what amounted to be a breezeway. They all ordered beer and then a whiskey.

Then it occurred to the Kitten that she had no money. She hadn't needed it out in the wild, but now that she was back in the "settlements," as Cheyenne called them, she would need spending money. The Sumi brothers listened to her dilemma and suggested that they could cover any expenses that she might have. She was slightly uncomfortable with that and, leaving the two mountain men with their drinks, she began looking for a job. Walking around the pleasant little town and trailed by her always-present wolf pup, she soon found one.

A large sign said, "Waitress wanted." She discovered that the job was in the hotel restaurant. It was a grand old building constructed in the style of old Mexico. Inside, it was spacious, dark, and cool. It seemed a nice enough place to work and she was to start the next day. But first a wonderful bath and then some new clothes.

The Kitten went to ask the old boys if they wanted to go along on her shopping spree. "Hell, yes," they said, and seeing as they were paying for it, they felt they should have a say in what she bought. She winked at them and giggled. It was to be like Christmas. They all were wearing big grins.

The trio ruffled a few feathers when they walked into the ladies' wear shop. They were all wearing buckskin and carrying Winchesters, short guns and knives, not exactly the average customer. The Kitten had bathed but the old boys were still rank from the trail.

Suffice it to say they all three had a high old time of it. The Kitten tried on many things and then stripped right in front of the old boys and tried on some more things, some of which none of the three had ever seen before. This behavior promptly emptied the store of the other lady shoppers and prompted old Hal to explain to the much embarrassed store clerk that it was all right for the old boys to be witness to these proceedings as they were her "fathers."

They purchased an all-new wardrobe for their "daughter." They bought a lot of white cotton lady's stuff and some colorful skirts and blouses for the girl. The old boys couldn't remember when they had more fun spending money plus the fact they got to see the Kitten in a different outfit each day. They quit calling her Squaw Girl and started calling her Little Kitten.

The Kitten was colorful and fancy with her low cut peasant blouses and brightly colored skirts. Some days she tied ribbons in her hair. She was always cheerful and great to look at.

She worked breakfast, lunch, and dinner, with time off in between and she had Sundays off. The old boys were two of her best customers. Nobody got fresh with the Kitten with the grizzly old boys standing guard on their property.

Meanwhile, the brothers found a place for them all to stay, with corrals for the critters. They planned to be there for just a short while and then move on south into Mexico. They reasoned that fall was just around the corner, and as this was still the "high country," they wanted to be long gone before the first snow fall.

The Kitten was glad to learn that she could still waitress if necessary, and though they had plenty of money she had mostly done it for fun. She said, "Working there helped to civilize her." And it probably did. She bathed every day and even cleaned under her fingernails. Wolf continued to sniff at her suspiciously and the Sumi brothers were delighted with their fancy companion. They bathed at least once a week for her, not for themselves, so as not to embarrass her.

Wolf had to make some adjustments to the Kitten's having a job where he couldn't go. So he did. He hid under a table and glared at the world of diners. He was an unseen guard dog. The three weeks were without incident and the travelers once more hit the trail.

They liked No Name and that part of Arizona but it was still up high and they wanted to be out of there when winter came. They hoped to find a town in old Mexico just like No Name, only not as high up, one where they could loaf through a warm and lazy winter.

Cheyenne

CHAPTER THIRTY-FOUR

While the three travelers were happily riding south, Cheyenne Williams was as angry as an old bear. He was angrily and doggedly following the trio. He kept finding where they had been, and most often with great difficulty. Tracking and backtracking an old trail is one of the most tedious, painstaking, and arduous endeavor, that anyone can attempt. Cheyenne was good but he was tired and so was his horse. He kept saying that no one was worth it. The ungrateful so and so. Yet he wouldn't or couldn't give up.

He knew he was getting close to finding the Kitten. People remembered the odd threesome when he inquired but mostly they remembered the beautiful girl and the ever-present wolf pup that was beginning to get some size to him. Cheyenne Williams had even passed up "supplies" on more than one occasion to avoid delay in his search for the Kitten. This was not like him. He was changing and he hated himself for it; he hated the

Kitten for it; he hated the two mountain men she was traveling with, and besides that he was beginning to hate the whole world.

He was coming to realize just how much the Kitten meant to him and worse still was the gnawing fear that he was, quite possibly, realizing it too late.

The man was driven and obsessed.

Watch out world!

Cheyenne rode into a hick town, and went to the only hotel to inquire if the clerk had seen the three travelers. The slimy clerk stalled to see some green by saying, "Maybe yes, and maybe no."

Cheyenne reached across the counter with his left hand and grabbed the fellow by his skinny neck, lifted the man up and pulled him back across the counter, and showing him the big knife, cut one of the man's nostrils in the blink of an eye. The little man screamed, "Yes," so loud he woke the town loafers who were sleeping on the porch.

"When, you idiot?"

"Three weeks back."

Then Cheyenne dropped him to the floor in a heap.

"Give me a room."

"Yes, sir, any room you want."

"I'll be back after I find a bottle."

Cheyenne brought back two girls with

him and booze for all.

The girls were delighted with the evening and he felt better after taking on "supplies," but it still failed to cheer him up for long.

He left early the next morning still following the nearly cold trail of the girl and two mountain men. A week later he arrived in No Name to discover they had left only three days before.

This good news really cheered him up for the first time in months.

He stayed two days in the very hotel where the Kitten had worked as a waitress. Her replacement was a willowy blonde. Cheyenne's dinner was interrupted when a local loud mouth came in an ordered the girl to quit work early as he was taking her dancing at a nearby saloon.

The blonde, who was not the best waitress in the whole wide world, was being bullied into a relationship by the local fast gun. The man had even slapped her a time or two, but not in front of Cheyenne. Cheyenne learned the girl had no family here to speak up for her, so he offered to have a talk with the fellow. With further questioning, he learned the girl would have preferred to be left alone by this local, fast gun, loud mouth.

After his dinner, Cheyenne went to the

saloon to have "a talk" with the fellow. The bartender pointed out the man seated at a table alone, apparently waiting for the blonde to show up. Cheyenne sat down at the man's table and said, "She's not coming."

"Just who the Hell are you?"

"I'm your worst nightmare."

"She'll come if she knows what's good for her."

"She already knows what's good for her, and you aren't it."

The man was used to being feared. He went for his gun and as his hand came up with the big .44, he suddenly dropped the gun to the floor. The man stared at the floor and saw his own trigger finger lying there along side his gun. Then he looked at his hand and then back at the floor again. He couldn't believe what had happened. The man was in shock when he said, "It wasn't supposed to be like this."

He was a known shooter. People feared him.

"Wrong, That was then. This is now."

Cheyenne wiped his huge knife on the man's sleeve and whispered to him, "If you ever mistreat a lady again, I'll come back and cut off your whole hand."

"This man needs a doctor," he said, as he was leaving.

Few people were even aware of what had

taken place.

Cheyenne Williams escorted the grateful, pretty, willowy blonde to his hotel and took on more "supplies." They were both glad the waitress had quit work early. It gave them more time.

Cheyenne

CHAPTER THIRTY-FIVE

Cheyenne Williams rested up at the hotel in No Name with the yellow haired waitress and his big stud horse rested up in the corrals out in back with a flaxen maned mare. It was a time of good food and plenty of rest for each of them. Things were looking up. A few more days of this kind of duty and they would be ready to travel again.

Williams had learned the direction the Sumi men and the Kitten had taken, and now he believed it was only a matter of a few days until he would find them. The weather was warm and the country was much lower now, as they traveled south, through vast fields of fragrant wild flowers, into old Mexico.

The mountain men had pushed hard for the warmer climates, and several days later, they all four met in a quiet little town, well below the border, called San Raphael. San Raphael was the center of a large vineyard area where the people took great pride in their wines.

The Kitten and the Sumi brothers were

sampling some of the recent harvest at an outdoor cantina. They were sitting in the shade of a grape arbor, having lunch and a glass of red wine, when Cheyenne rode up.

The Kitten was the first to see him and she ran out into the street to greet him. She called his name and ran up to his horse. He was down in a second and embraced her. He just held her and she hung on to him and wouldn't let go. She laughed and cried and then she laughed and cried some more. She buried her face into his chest

"You did come after me. You did come. I had almost given up. Oh, Cheyenne, I'm so happy. You did come after me." Still she wouldn't release him from her iron grip.

"You came to find me." She was jumping up and down. "You came to find me, after all. At last, you came for me."

No one had ever seen the Kitten so happy. Her mood was infectious. Cheyenne was wearing a big grin and still holding her. She was dancing up and down with tears in her eyes while she still hugged him. The Sumi brothers came running over to meet Cheyenne. They also had tears in their eyes, and at the same time, they were wearing great big smiles on their faces. Cheyenne Williams was happier than he had ever been in his entire life, and he was very puzzled by his depth of emotion over this girl, girl-woman, woman-girl, woman! He was certainly in the best mood he had been in months.

The three men greeted one another, and shook hands all around. Then the Kitten tried to hug all three at the same time.

"I'm so happy. I'm so happy."

With a bright smile and tears in her eyes, she said, "I love you all."

The men all had a similar thought at about the same time. If she likes him, them, that much, then that's good enough for everyone. Now the Kitten had a larger family and three very capable protectors.

The group broke apart and then the Kitten gave Cheyenne a great big kiss, a long passionate one. She fully intended to build a fire under this big lug. Cheyenne Williams was surprised for the second time. The Little Kitten had grown into a lioness. He was more than pleased.

Cheyenne

CHAPTER THIRTY SIX

Cheyenne checked into the same hotel, but got his own room. He discovered the Kitten was disappointed because she wanted him to stay in her room, and she said so.

He still didn't see her as "supplies" so he did his firm drill. He insisted on having his own room. She was perturbed but went along with it with a friendly pout. She was determined to get his attention but she had waited this long and she thought to herself that she could wait a little longer. Not much, but a little.

The four of them settled down to the good and lazy life. They were resting up from the trail. They rested their bodies, and they pampered their stomachs with good food and drink. They lazed about in the hammocks in the courtyard just off their rooms, on warm sunny mornings, and in the shade of the two big old cottonwood trees that grew there, in the hot afternoons. They frequently swam together in the buff in the stream near the village and shocked the women who were there to wash their clothes. The padre spoke to them and they agreed to swim in a less populated area. Some of the women were envious of the Kitten's freedom and others were envious of her handsome North Americano.

In the evenings they dined at the hotel or the local cantina and afterward they danced or watched others dancing to the lively music. They drank beer or wine or tequila and sometimes all three. It was a great good time for awhile.

The Kitten was a little miffed at sleeping alone, but she was so happy to have Cheyenne back again that she didn't let on. But the Sumi brothers had learned to read her pretty well by this time, and they well knew how she felt. They were wondering if they should intervene in some way. Neither of them knew anything about women but they did know their Kitten was not quite happy about Cheyenne. They also thought, and they guessed right, that Cheyenne Williams would be the last man on earth to seek advice from any man, especially about a woman. For the time being they would just have to wait and watch.

San Raphael was the perfect place for them to winter. It offered holiday celebrations, festivals, and high holy days about every ten days. The villagers were hung over and cleaning up after the last event and at the same time, others were getting ready for the next occasion.

Cheyenne Williams went back to his old pursuits and found there were plenty of "supplies" in this lively village. He was nearly a model citizen because he was leaving the married ladies alone. He cracked very few heads, and those he did belonged to jealous boyfriends. So almost nobody cared, and certainly not the law.

Cheyenne was the picture of contentment. He had plenty of gold. He had "supplies" and the Kitten was safely chaperoned by the Sumi boys. Life was good, perhaps better than in a long time.

Not so with the Kitten. She was remembering why she had left him in the first place. She had the blahs. Knowing the cause of her mood, she decided to make a drastic move.

It was early December and she had noticed the group was getting restless with all of the good living, so she brought home a bottle of expensive whiskey and proposed that they all go to California at the end of the week. The brothers were in favor of the idea and Cheyenne reluctantly agreed. She didn't tell them, but if they had refused she was ready to go to California on her own. The week would give them time to pack, get the horses shod and buy what trail things they needed. They would need to purchase one more packhorse.

The bottle was passed around and she saw to it that Cheyenne had more than his share. That night when Cheyenne went to bed she intended to be in it. The trick was to get him to stay put and not go looking for "supplies."

Once, when she thought he was thinking about leaving, she asked him for his opinion about the white elk skin dress she had been making—the one he had seen a few times before, but at the time was still unfinished. Even though it was only ten weeks, the Kitten had matured more than somewhat in the time she had been separated from Cheyenne.

She went to her room and put on the beautiful and very sexy dress, which just came to three inches above her mid thigh. She also put on her knee high Apache type legging-moccasins complete with two concealed throwing knives, and a garland of fresh wild flowers that she had made. She placed the garland of flowers on her head like a crown. Then she put on the dangle earrings she had made from bright, light blue beads and small feathers. The earrings hung down beside her pretty neck. The elk dress had a small amount of beadwork over the left breast. At the top in back, it had a high shirt collar. In front, at the neck, it was cut wide and low to show a delicious amount of ripe firm breast and some very impressive cleavage. The upper part of the two- piece dress, tapered in and stopped to show a four inch bare mid-rift at the waist, hugged her body like a second skin. She wore nothing under it.

When she walked out into the courtyard, all of the people present became silent. Cheyenne and the Sumi brothers first gaped, then stood up and applauded. So did most of the locals, both men and women. They all knew they were seeing a woman of rare beauty. The Kitten looked every inch a queen and her bright smile dazzled everyone. She was the picture of health and elegance. She was looking at Cheyenne the whole time and was so pleased with his reaction, that she had tears in her eyes.

Cheyenne Williams was astounded. He knew he had just witnessed the metamorphosis of a goddess. The girl had really pulled his heartstrings and he went to her. He hugged her and said, "Kitten, I love you." Then he kissed her tenderly, picked her up and carried her to his room. They were followed by the melodic strains of a romantic Mexican ballad, played on several guitars.

That night the Kitten was very successful in all of her nocturnal endeavors and

Cheyenne

Cheyenne Williams found more “supplies” than he could handle.

THE END

ABOUT THE AUTHOR

Photo by Rene Salmon

K. IMUS

K. Imus is a man of many places and careers. He holds a B.A., B.Ed., and an M.F.A. in sculpture from the University of Washington. As a college professor, he taught life drawing, painting, sculpture, and art appreciation. The major theme of his own art focuses on the female form. K. Imus is a skier, lives in Sun Valley, Idaho, and returns to Kihei, Maui each year to swim and play tennis. During the summer he lives on his 35 foot sailboat in Seattle, Washington.

At times, K. Imus has led the life of a vagabond adventurer. He quit high school at age 16, and served on a troop ship in the Pacific during World War II. Later, while he was in Japan, he was drafted by the U.S. Army to serve in the Korean War.

He completed high school and went on to college. By age 21 he had traveled to Europe seven times. As a vagabond adventurer, he has skippered sailing yachts, fished Alaska, sailed French Polynesia, including Tahiti and Bora Bora, worked as a migrant farm laborer, worked the docks in Seattle and Alaska, drove a taxi, and visited much of the world in the Merchant Marine. In addition, he worked an alpaca and llama ranch near Melbourne, Australia, sailed a square rigger, worked as a horse wrangler for an outfitter in Montana, and cowboyed on the Crooked H Ranch in Arizona.

K. Imus published his first novel, ***Zero Smith***, in 1996. His second novel, ***Galway***, is also a western.